LONG RIDIN' MAN

They call him 'Hunter'. There is one man in particular for whom he searches: the man who destroyed his family. Trailing the killer, Hunter finds himself in a booming town short of one deputy sheriff: in need of cash, he pins on the badge. But the folk of Cimarron begin to wonder just who they've hired as their peacemaker. Once Hunter discovers why the town needed a fast gun so urgently, the odds are that it will be too late for him to get out alive . . .

JAKE DOUGLAS

LONG RIDIN' MAN

Complete and Unabridged

LINFORD
Leicester

First published in Great Britain in 2014 by
Robert Hale Limited
London

First Linford Edition
published 2015
by arrangement with
Robert Hale Limited
London

A catalogue record for this book is available
from the British Library.

ISBN 978–1–4448–2535–0

Published by
F. A. Thorpe (Publishing)
Anstey, Leicestershire

Set by Words & Graphics Ltd.
Anstey, Leicestershire
Printed and bound in Great Britain by
T. J. International Ltd., Padstow, Cornwall

This book is printed on acid-free paper

1

Line of Fire

She just seemed to materialize out of the fug and noise of the saloon bar.

One moment he was alone at the corner table, the next, she was standing there — a bar-girl with silvered hair piled up in curls, of indeterminate age, and wearing a once-elegant gown that would show plenty of cleavage, and a smile as false as a desert mirage.

'You look kinda lonesome, cowboy.' Her voice was almost smooth, but roughened around the edges, likely from working long hours in the turgid air of saloons — not to mention the effect from the 'drinks' the barkeep would make for her — at the customer's expense.

He glanced up, hat pushed back enough to show the trail-gaunted face with its four days' stubble. And the steady, pale bullet-grey eyes that somehow reminded her of — well, she didn't really want to think about what they reminded her of. She already felt a touch of a shiver.

'I've company enough.' His voice was deep, weary, verging on harshness.

She widened her blue eyes and the false smile spread as she mimed looking at the empty chairs around his table. 'Where?'

'Right here.'

She brightened then and placed a hand with painted fingernails on the back of one of the empty chairs. 'Oh! You mean me.'

His boot reached behind a chair leg so she couldn't move it and, as her smile faded, he said, 'I mean *me*.'

Her face straightened and the eyes slitted. She leaned down a little, flag-red lips curling slightly, even allowing him a glimpse of cleavage. 'I could take that as a personal insult!'

'Go right ahead.' He sounded totally indifferent.

The silver head came closer and he got a whiff of cheap perfume and whiskey as she said with a vicious touch, 'Suppose I call a houseman?'

'Suit yourself.'

'And what will you do then?' she almost sneered.

'Probably shoot him.' He wasn't even looking at her now.

She reared back, a hand going to her powdered throat, some blood draining from her shocked face. 'Sweet Mary! You . . . you got some kinda problem with me?'

'Not you — *him*!' He came swiftly to his feet, left arm thrusting her shoulder roughly. She gave a small scream as she staggered away from the table.

But it was lost in the crash of the sixgun in his hand, blasting past her at a long-haired man half-rising from his chair at the next table. The bullet struck him just below the throat, knocking him over violently. As he went backwards he triggered the sawn-off shotgun he had been holding beneath the table. Wood splinters flew, thrumming, and playing cards erupted like violently swirling snowflakes. The concussion of the shot rent the pall of tobacco smoke and showed the three other men who had been sitting at the table diving away in all directions, trying to dodge the flying shards of shattered bottles and glasses. If the shotgun hadn't been on the rise when it fired, they might have all been crippled — or worse — by now.

There was a mass exodus — or attempted exodus: running men and screaming saloon girls jamming the batwings entrance and the narrow side doorway. Everyone seemed to be yelling, but nothing intelligible, just sound.

The cowboy was still on his feet, smoking gun in one hand, while he grabbed the stunned silver-haired girl by a flabby upper arm, steadying her, pushing her down into one of the spare chairs that still stood at the table.

'Sorry to be so rough, but you were in my line of fire.'

She merely stared, eyes wide, a rapid pulse fluttering at her throat as her heart thundered against her ribs. He nodded and backed against the wall a few feet from the table. The man he had shot sprawled, very still, a snake of blood writhing from beneath his body. The shotgun lay smoking a couple of feet away. The cowboy swept his alert gaze around the room but no further danger threatened him.

The few men left in the big room showed no inclination to butt in on this ranny's business.

It was a different matter, though, when the sheriff arrived. 'Someone get the sawbones and tell me what happened.'

They all began speaking at once as he jostled his way through the crowd. He was a man on the wrong side of forty — not too far, though — and he had a hard stare with flecked brown eyes that seemed to drill clear through anyone they touched in passing.

When they came to rest on the

cowboy, the lawman nodded to the smoking gun the man still held.

'Guess you did the shootin'.'

'Part — ' He indicated the Colt. 'Not the shotgun.'

'You had a good reason, of course.'

The Colt gestured to the dead man and when it moved the muzzle of the lawman's gun lifted slightly, about where it would need to be to put a bullet into the cowboy's head. 'Careful how you wave that gun about, mister.'

The cowboy gave no indication he had heard. 'Heard him cock the shotgun he was holding under the table.'

'And why would he do that?'

'I been trailing that 'breed for nigh on eight hundred miles.'

'And tonight you caught up with him. Private affair, of course.' When the cowboy nodded briefly, the sheriff shook his head slightly. 'Thing is, this is my bailiwick. You bring your troubles here and they become mine, too.'

'No trouble here — the son of a bitch

is dead. That's an end to it.'

The sheriff moved closer to the cowboy now. 'Well, no one except the 'breed seems to've been hurt bad, so I'd be obliged if you'd leather that gun.'

'How about you do the same?'

The lawman almost smiled then, shook his head slowly. 'You're a sassy sonuver, ain't you? But OK. How about we do it together . . . now.'

The guns slid smoothly into their respective holsters, but the lawman's came out again so swiftly that the cowboy wasn't certain if the man had even holstered it at all, however briefly.

He stiffened. 'Now that's what I call pullin' a fast one.'

The sheriff shrugged, unsmiling. 'Can't take a chance with a man who can shoot quick enough to beat the fall of a shotgun's hammer. That's real fast.' He leaned closer, studying the cowboy's trail-ravaged face. 'You got the eyes of a hunter, mister. That what you are? A man-hunter?'

The cowboy tensed, green eyes

narrowing. 'Told you I been hunting that 'breed for months.'

'Yeah. The tag kinda fits you well, don't it? Seen you ride in just on sundown — a careful man, I told myself. Watched you dismount and walk in here. You move like a cat stalkin' prey . . . Reminded me of a hunter.'

'We met before?' The cowboy spoke tautly, his whole body rigid. When the lawman shook his head, he said, 'Then how come I get the notion you're telling me you recognize me?'

'That what I'm doin'?'

'Don't sound so innocent — My *name's* Hunter. Seems like your smart way of lettin' me know you know that.'

'What's the rest of it?' The lawman didn't deny the cowboy was right.

'Just Hunter.'

'Uh-huh. Might've seen your picture somewhere.'

'Not on any Wanted dodger.'

'We-ell, I ain't sure about that.'

'You got a name? Or you keeping that secret?'

8

'McAdam.'

Hunter's eyebrows arched briefly. 'Foster McAdam? Hell, no wonder you got that gun up so fast!'

'You're no slouch yourself.' The gun muzzle jerked slightly towards the dead man. The hard eyes were steady now on the stubbled face. 'Mebbe you're thinking you're faster'n me.'

'Mebbe — seems a wise thing to do.'

McAdam nodded slowly. 'You're right. No sense goin' up agin a man thinkin' *he* might be faster than you. Seein' as you're still walkin' around, I guess you've been right — so far.'

'So far.'

McAdam's look was different now, more respectful. 'Right again. It won't be forever. Always gotta be a time when there's someone who can shade you. You kinda interest me, *amigo*. Best come on down to the jailhouse.'

He made a small ushering movement with his free hand but the cowboy didn't move.

'Anyone here'll tell you it was a

fair-and-square shoot-out, McAdam.'

'Shoot-out? Hardly call it that, would you?'

'The 'breed recognized me, knew I was here to kill him. He'd've blasted me from under the table if I hadn't shot him first.'

McAdam swung his head towards the trio who had been at the same table with the 'breed. 'You fellers got any argument with that?'

'No, sir!' said one tall *hombre*, rubbing at blood spots on his left leg where some buckshot had peppered him. 'I was figurin' on throwin' in my cards just to get away from the table. That 'breed was expectin' trouble, all right.'

The others murmured and nodded agreement.

'Well, it sounds like that's the way it was.' The lawman looked steadily at Hunter. 'But we'll go down to the jailhouse anyway . . . I want you on hand while I check through some of my dodgers.'

'I already told you, I ain't — '

'I *know* what you told me!' McAdam's voice was sharp now, his whole body showing his tension. 'If it's true, you got no worries.'

'Wouldn't say that, Sheriff. I'm a long-ridin' man. I don't like to be walled in, temporary or otherwise.'

The lawman gave him that steady, almost unreadable stare and jerked his gun again. 'I can savvy that. C'mon, walk down to the law office with me anyway, might even find you a cup of java while you wait.'

'Not in any cell.'

'Don't push things too far.' The sheriff's face and tone were bone-hard now.

Still Hunter hesitated, but when McAdam started to cock the gun hammer, he lifted his hands out from his sides, settled his hat and took a dollar from his shirt pocket. He flicked it towards the silver-haired goodtime girl who was still standing close by. She blinked in surprise as

11

she caught the coin.

'For the drink I didn't get to buy you.'

Her smile was wide and warm now. 'Hey! You come on back sometime, cowboy. This just might buy you more than a lousy drink!'

He winked and stepped past the sheriff who raised his eyebrows at the girl and followed Hunter towards the batwings.

He holstered his gun as they pushed through the crowd and stepped out into the night.

The lawman pointed the way to the law office where a lamp glowed dully behind a smeared window.

'Walk just one step ahead of me.'

Hunter gave him a sharp look. 'I heard you were careful.'

'That's how come I'm headin' towards old age and retirement — slow, but sure.'

McAdam sounded as if he meant that and Hunter did as he was told, stepped ahead, but slightly to one side, the right side, so that his gunarm would have clear space to move — if necessary.

He heard the sheriff chuckle softly. 'Talkin' about bein' careful . . . '

2

Badge-Toter

Hunter had rolled and smoked two cigarettes before McAdam had finished shuffling through the thick pile of Wanted dodgers on his battered desk — twice.

The sheriff sat back in his chair without comment, took a well-used pipe from his shirt pocket and packed the charred bowl from a small worked-leather humidor on his desk. Hunter waited patiently, looking around the small neat office again. Everything seemed to be exactly in place — the pigeonholes that held the posters and other papers were clear of dust, the contents lined up, the edges neatly squared. There were no untidy splashes showing around the inkstand and the pens lay in their shallow grooves, nib-to-handle. Curtains on the single window — *and* — *well, well!* There was a small vase on the desk with a bunch of colourful flowers that Hunter couldn't put a name to, though he had seen them growing both in the wild and along pathways leading to church doors and grouped in cottage gardens.

He started a little when he looked up and saw the sheriff smiling around the stem of his pipe as he puffed smoke in aromatic clouds. The lawman nodded his head towards the flowers.

'Wife likes things neat and tidy — has a green thumb. Grows all our own fresh vegetables, so we eat well. Flowers are a bonus.'

Hunter nodded: he hadn't thought of McAdam as being married for some reason — and the man looked older now his hat was off, displaying a half-bald scalp.

'You didn't find me on any of your dodgers.'

'No — not under that name, anyways.'

There may have been a sly glint in McAdam's eye as he said that and Hunter just cut off his retort in time.

'Only name I use,' he said equably. 'No need for aliases.'

'Uh-huh. Well, to be honest it don't mean much — I've remembered where I've seen your picture.'

Hunter waited, drew on his cigarette, exhaled, waiting McAdam out. *Damned if he was going to ask 'where'* . . . even though he couldn't think 'where' just the same.

'Be a few years back now, in a newspaper called the *Border Legend*. You recollect it?

'Used to be published in El Paso, went broke. Bit of a rag . . . hard to believe half of what they printed.'

McAdam grinned, showing tobacco-stained, crooked bottom teeth, but surprisingly clean and intact top ones. 'Aw, I take most of what gets into print with a grain of salt, but when they put a man's picture along with the words, I usually figure there's some truth in what they have to say.' He drew deeply on his pipe, exhaled slowly, watching Hunter with those brown-flecked eyes. 'Like when a man breaks out of a so-called impregnable prison down around Chihuahua — outruns the *Rurales* and half the Mexican army, *then* walks back openly across the bridge from Juarez into El Paso — well, it sounds like a little more'n fiction to me, so many details.'

Hunter merely shrugged, locking gazes with the lawman who smiled wryly. 'Sounds far-fetched, you ask me.'

'You done it, though, didn't you? I don't recall why you were in the prison but you're the only one who ever got out and lived to tell about it.'

'I was riding with a wild bunch. Just hoo-rawin' a few Mexes here and there, bunch of us lettin' off steam after the war ended, until our leader got ambitious — or greedy, more like. He took on a job for us that involved assassination of some Mex *politico*.'

McAdam frowned. 'That wasn't in the *Legend*.'

'No. Had to be hushed up. Big upset when it went wrong. Someone claimed it was our new Union Government up here that was behind it. Things got a mite touchy at those levels. Anyway, made no nevermind. One of the *politico*'s mistresses unmanned him and he bled to death.' Hunter ended with a shrug.

The sheriff waited for more, finally said, 'Well, how the hell did you bust out of a place with a reputation like that prison? *Hacienda Putrido* they called it, didn't they?'

Hunter smiled crookedly. 'Yeah, and it sure was rotten — all the way. Wasn't a sane guard in the place. Someone said they combed the asylums and jails for all the homicidal maniacs they could find.'

'Don't sound like no rest home — but how the *hell* did you get out?'

'Complicated. Involved me takin' a certain drug that made me look dead.

18

Wrapped me up in a burlap sheet with four corpses. Had to cut my way out after them lazy sonuvers dropped us into the river. I almost drowned.'

'Judas!' The lawman sat up straighter in his chair, pipe frozen halfway to his mouth. 'That must've — well, hell, I don't know that I could've gone through with anythin' like that.'

'You'd be surprised at what you'd do after six months in that hellhole.'

'Well? That all you gonna say?'

Hunter spread his hands. 'I'm here.'

McAdam snorted, glared. 'How come there wasn't a lot more made of your escape? I mean, it must've been mighty rough, a good story for a rag like that *Legend*.'

'Hell, it was, but our government put an official clamp on it for political reasons. The *Legend* was stupid enough to try to defy 'em — and — so, they went broke.'

McAdam nodded gently. 'Yeah. Heard those things can happen. Hunter, you lookin' for work now you've squared

19

away with that 'breed — whatever he done to you?'

There was an interrogating lift to the sheriff's last words as he looked hopefully at Hunter.

'No great mystery. He killed my wife.'

'Aaaah! Sorry — I've been a lawman for a long time and I'm just naturally curious. You needn't go into detail . . . '

He let the words trail off as he saw the haunted look on Hunter's gaunt face. The words were barely audible as the big man added, 'And my baby daughter.'

McAdam went very still. He was surprised when he found his sudden grip had snapped the stem of his pipe. His mouth opened but he suddenly got to his feet, dropping the pipe's remains into a wastepaper basket, went to a cupboard and came back with a bottle of whiskey and two glasses. Silently he poured drinks to the brims and held one out towards Hunter, whose mind was obviously rolling back through the years, stirring mighty uncomfortable memories.

He took the drink, raised his haunted eyes to the lawman, stared a long moment, then nodded briefly, tossed down the whiskey. McAdam drank his in two gulps.

'Three years since it happened,' Hunter said quietly. 'And — and it galls the *hell* outta me because I . . . I can't quite . . . recollect exactly how they . . . looked!'

'That kinda thing does happen, I hear,' McAdam said. 'Nothin' to feel guilty about.'

Hunter went on as if the lawman hadn't spoken.

'I guess I concentrated so hard on finding that murderin' bastard I . . . I almost forgot why I wanted to kill him so badly. Just wanted to get it done.'

'And you did.'

'Then why don't I feel better about it?'

'It's the kinda thing that takes a helluva lot out of a man — especially one who's basically decent himself.'

Hunter snapped his head up. 'You can't know that.'

'I'm a pretty good judge of men, Hunter, that's why I'm offering you the job of being my deputy.'

'Me?'

'I can use one — a good man. I reckon you're him.'

'But this is just a jerkwater town — you wouldn't need a deputy here.'

'I will do. Town's about to boom. See, some of the men in town figured that what the big spreads back beyond the Cataracts needed was an easy way up to the meat markets. Some of 'em got together, pooled their money and resources and finally blew a pass through Cimarron Canyon. Took 'em well into winter. Helluva job, gave a lotta men winter work, though. They'll have it cleared in time for this season's trail drives and there'll be cattle herds from three counties all comin' through here. We're right at the entrance to the pass, any other way would take weeks longer, drivin' steers over the range and through the kinda country that's out there, wearin' 'em down to hide an' bone.'

Hunter's face was blank and then he nodded slowly. 'Yeah, through here'd be the best way down to the Rambia trail and the meat buyers all right, but who pays for the pass? Must've cost plenty.'

'Yeah, but the same men as made the pass'll get their money back all right — and after only a few seasons.'

Hunter looked up sharply, then nodded slowly. 'Head tax?'

'Only way. User pays — and those ranchers might bitch a mite, but they'll soon see they're gettin' a bargain in the end. A few cents a head'll get their cattle through in top condition, means better prices — or that's the theory.'

'Sounds fair. But, I dunno, McAdam — deputy? I've never had a badge-toter's job before . . . What's it pay?'

'Fifty a month, plus keep — maybe.'

Hunter arched his eyebrows.

'Town council have to approve it.

They're mostly businesmen and they all got an eye out for the dollars they can see pourin' in with those herds. Also, most of 'em invested somethin' in makin' the pass. What d'you say?'

'Place is gonna be lively, I can see that, but totin' a badge just don't seem like me. Then again, I'm broke.' He paused, half-squinted at the lawman. 'I guess if I don't like it, I don't need to stay.'

'There'll be a contract,' McAdam said flatly. 'And the council will hold you to it. You want to think about it overnight?'

Hunter pursed his lips. 'All right, I'll sleep on it. There a decent rooming-house that'll gimme credit?'

McAdam stood, reaching for his hat. 'I'll take you to the place where you'll be staying if you pin on a deputy's star. Called Rosa's Rooming-house. Think you'll like it.'

As he stood, Hunter said slowly, 'You get many applyin' for the deputy's job?'

McAdam looked up quickly. 'No, but

the chairman of the council, Will Bardon, has sort of recommended his brother-in-law, one Ollie Revell.'

Again the pause. Hunter waited, face neutral.

'I've used Ollie a couple of times. Good man for settling a brawl, but — no one he brought in, and he brought in a *lot*, ever had more than a few cents in their pockets — some not even that. And when they sobered up, they all swore they never drank their wallets dry ... but they'd been gun-whipped and were groggy and — well there you are.' McAdam smiled wryly. 'Ollie's a bit too eager, enjoys gun-whippin'. Not anyone I'd like for a permanent deputy, but I gotta tread carefully: council pays my wages, too.'

'Don't count too much on me being permanent — not till I see how I like it.'

The sheriff's gaze was steady. 'If you sign our contract ... '

Hunter nodded. 'We'll have to see, huh? Now, where's this rooming-house? I've got my appetite back.'

3

'Not This Man!'

The name of the rooming-house was 'Rosa's', but the woman-owner Sheriff McAdam introduced Hunter to was called Tess Deacon.

Hunter paused in offering his hand, frowning, puzzled, when he saw Tess Deacon's face.

Just for an instant there, she looked like she was thinking of killing him . . . and she ignored his proffered hand.

McAdam noticed Hunter's reaction, if not the woman's, and said amiably, 'Rosa was kind of — odd. Half-Mexican, outlived four husbands, and when the fifth prospect came along, she sold the rooming-house and had him take her back to Mexico . . . Tess runs a fine place, good grub, clean sheets.'

His voice trailed off as he saw the

woman and Hunter staring at each other. He cleared his throat. 'You two know each other by any chance . . . ?'

Both started shaking their heads. Hunter had never seen the woman before — and he was certain he would remember because she was a fine-looking female, tall and willowy, with a kind of narrow face that wasn't pinched, but smooth-skinned and well-made — if that was the right word when talking about a lady's features.

Her mouth was wide and soft-looking, her jaw showing a touch of stubbornness, her nose small but not too small, and her eyes lake blue, hair flaxen and curly. Impressed, he once again started to offer his hand but she made no move to match the gesture.

'Hunter?' she said in a quiet voice and with a level look. 'I heard of a man who used that name a couple of years ago. In Arizona, a place near Tombstone if I recollect.'

'Saguaro Springs?' Hunter offered, frowning a little now. *He still didn't recognize her . . . but the Springs was where he had been at that time and . . .*

'Yes!' The lovely eyes narrowed. 'It was you!'

McAdam looked from one to the other. 'What happened in Saguaro Springs?' he asked carefully.

She looked hard at Hunter but he remained silent.

'I had a small haberdashery store there — on the corner of Main and Post Street.' Tess paused but Hunter said nothing, his face worked blank now. 'It was a wild town, with some of the riffraff from Tombstone drifting through and — causing trouble.'

Hunter tensed slightly as Tess's face tightened.

'You remember, all right, don't you?' Her voice had an edge of breathlessness now.

'Nothin' too specific,' he allowed. 'But like you say, some of the scum kicked out of Tombstone made their way to Saguaro, hardcases just looking for trouble.'

'And finding it! Like challenging anyone to a gun-fight! Just bravado mainly . . . ' Her voice was taking on a bitter edge and McAdam frowned, eyes flicking sharply.

'Sounds plenty rough,' he opined. 'No law?'

Tess looked hard at Hunter, arched her eyebrows, inclining her head a little in an invitation for him to reply.

'Two drunks braced me,' Hunter said steadily. 'Mean and stubborn as hell, wouldn't let me step around or just walk away. They pushed it until I had no choice but to draw.'

'And you killed them both!' The girl's eyes blazed.

'They'd've killed me.'

'But you could see they were drunk!'

'Crazy drunk! Dyin' to prove to each other just how tough they were. Lady, I don't like gunfights, but when there's no way out but to shoot, I shoot to kill.'

Her bosom was heaving now and her slim hands were clenched down at her sides. Without looking at McAdam she said, 'I think you'd better find some other place for your man to stay, Foster.'

'If he takes the deputy's job, he'll need somewhere permanant, Tess, and the council has recommended your place. You were the first to apply when council offered 'incentive', which means rental assistance and so on. A good deal of custom would come your way, too — '

'They were my brothers!' she blurted.

Hunter straightened another inch. 'Their name was Norman as I recall. Not Deacon.'

The blue eyes cold, she held up her left hand and her thumb wriggled the wedding ring on her third finger. 'Deacon is my married name! I'm a widow.'

Hunter nodded slightly, not having noticed the ring before. 'I'm sorry it happened, ma'am, but I wasn't about to stand still and let them two make a salt-shaker outa me.'

'Sounds like it was self-defence,'

McAdam added. 'It's easily checked.' But apart from a scathing, passing look, Tess ignored the sheriff, her slitted gaze on Hunter.

'You'd been showing off your prowess with a gun all over town! Shooting whiskey glasses out of the air, splitting matches, punching holes in cards: boastful, provocative acts!' Her bosom heaved faster with rising emotion. 'You were looking for trouble and . . . and took advantage of my brothers.'

Hunter showed no signs of backing away from her fury. 'They were drunk enough to feel frisky and take on the world. I heard later they'd beat a man for his poker winnings just so they could buy a bottle of booze.' Swiftly he held up a hand as her eyes seemed to actually blaze at him. 'Whether it's true or not makes no nevermind now. They wanted to shoot me full of holes and I simply didn't aim for it to happen. As for me showing off my 'gun prowess', I was working: I've had to find jobs to keep me going while trailing that 'breed. I'd hired on to a travelling tent show to do a trick shooting act, popping cigarettes outa the mouths of pretty women, shootin' coins off drunks' noses — it was all mostly rigged: a stooge hiding with a length of thin twine yanking the coins off. I couldn't guarantee I wouldn't shoot the feller's nose off.'

'It's not funny!' she snapped, but there was a slight reticence as McAdam kept shaking his head.

'It was my job to go into a town a day ahead of the show with the smilin' gal ticket-seller, and a stooge to manipulate some of our tricks, make folk believe I really could shoot whiskey glasses outa the air at will, punch a hole through the ace of spades at ten paces. All done by exact timing on my part and the stooge's. It took plenty of practice, too, but it was all an act to get folk interested in comin' along to see the show when it arrived. It was carefully set up by the promoter. Hell, I'm not that good a shot! Your brothers fell for it like most others, but they were drunk enough, or stupid enough, to think they could out-shoot me anyway.'

There was a wet glisten to her eyes. Her fingers were absolutely white, she clenched her hands, so tightly. 'I don't want this man staying here, Foster!'

'Be reasonable, Tess. You know the town's over-flowin' with dozens of men looking to work the cattle drives.' He scratched at his ear, adding, 'Council won't be happy you refuse to take Hunter. They gave you preference, you know, and there can be a lotta extra business put your way.'

'I don't care!'

'Me, neither, Sheriff,' added Hunter, starting to turn away. 'I'd be afraid of finding rat poison in my stew.'

'Now there's a good suggestion!' Tess snapped.

'Cut it out!' McAdam sounded genuinely angry. 'Tess, you're a reasonable woman, two years ought to have taken the edge off your anger. Hunter here's explained how things were and from what I knew of Jake and Carl, they were hotheads and it wouldn't've been their first gunfight.'

'They were my brothers! Yes, they were hell-raisers, but they walked away from most gunfights! Except this one!'

Hunter touched a hand to his hatbrim. 'Like I said, ma'am, I'm sorry it happened. I hope you'll get over your upset. Sheriff, it's so long since I slept in a proper bed that another night roughin' it won't bother me. I'll swing a deal with the livery man and sleep in my hoss's stall. I'll call round in the morning and let you know if I want the job or not. 'Night — folks.'

He strode away and the girl tilted her chin but seemed to swallow whatever she'd intended to say when McAdam glared at her.

'Never seen you like this before, Tess.'

'I never thought I'd ever come face to face with the murderer of the only family I had left.'

He nodded. 'Yeah, it must've been damn upsettin', comin' so close after your husband was killed in that lumber-yard accident — but, Tess, that Hunter — he lost his wife and a baby daughter, murdered by that 'breed he killed tonight. Seems to me he's due a little compassion, too.'

Tess's face remained rigid, then softened slightly. 'Then you give it to him! You always were a softy at heart, Foster McAdam. That's why folk can never figure out how you make such a good lawman.'

'Just have strong beliefs, is all — and I'm prepared to stand up for 'em. Like Hunter, he — '

'Oh, damn Hunter! And you, too! I'm going to have enough trouble trying to sleep without you pushing your darn notions down my throat.'

'Tess, there's another thing: Will Bardon is pushin' me to take on Ollie Revell as my deputy — '

'Not that arrogant bully!'

The sheriff kept his face stern. 'Ollie's his brother-in-law, as you know. What I'm sayin', Tess, your place here is only a few doors from the saloon and that's where any trouble's gonna start, you can take my word on that.'

Tight-faced, she nodded jerkily. 'I agree, but it's never bothered us before.'

'Never been allowed to overflow this far. But this town is really gonna boom! We're gonna double the population in a few days. The most the council will finance is two deputies for me. Now, if Hunter decides he doesn't want the job, that leaves Ollie, and the council want at least one deputy, whoever he is, to board with you, so — '

'So he's close to the saloon. Yes, yes, I see that. But surely I have a say about who I accept as a boarder and who I don't!'

McAdam scratched at one ear. 'You'd think it'd work that way, but you know Will Bardon. Stubborn as a sierra goat. He was the one came up with the idea and now he's stuck with it. So, although Ollie's in the running, if Hunter says yes, he should be the one to have the room here.'

'Not that man! I won't have him under the same roof.'

'Then you'll get Ollie, like it or not.'

'Oh! For heaven's sake, Foster! You know damn well, and *I* do too, that you can talk Will Bardon around if you put your mind to it.'

'Tess, I'm in this too; I need a deputy close by to back me up . . . ' Then he smiled briefly, lowered his voice a little, adding, 'Not as spry as I like to make out.' He touched a hand to his hatbrim. 'Well, you think about it — it comes down to your choice, don't it?'

The door slammed and, as McAdam called a belated ' 'Night, Tess', through it, he smiled crookedly, before turning away and heading back up the street.

'Mac, ole pard,' he murmured, as he traipsed away, 'I reckon we're gonna be in for some interestin' times — if this Hunter takes a deputy's badge — *right* interestin'! And if he don't . . . Mebbe even more so!'

He whistled softly and added a little more speed to his pace.

Already he was beginning to feel the pressure of this born-again town.

4

Gunwhip

'Well, Lo-o-orrdee me! By Gall, soon's I heard that gut-hook 'breed was lyin' dead on the saloon floor, I says, 'The man who done that has the run of my stables! Yessir, *the run of 'em!*' Not to mention a swig of my moonshine . . . huh?'

Hunter shook his head: he felt kind of uneasy as the grey-bearded, pole-thin livery owner took off his battered hat and crumpled it between his knuckly hands. He then made a creaky bow — just a few inches — and waved the old hat.

'Mister — I hereby gives you the freedom of these here livery stables. You want to sleep in a stall for the night? Go right ahead. You got notions that come mornin' you'll be stackin' hay bales to pay for it? Forget 'em! Here, come on! Show you somethin' first.'

Hunter hesitated a moment as the man grabbed him by the shoulder and tugged. He went along, wondering what next. The hostler weaved between the stalls, most of which were taken, and stopped by one in shadow at the end of a line. His face was sober now and he was muttering something uncomplimentary in a bitter tone. He pointed to where a horse lay on the hay. It looked miserable from Hunter's angle and then he caught the whiff of blood and untended wounds.

'Yeah! That's it. Look closer, but you won't have to strain none to see what that lousy 'breed's guthook spurs've done to this poor hunk of crowbait.'

Hunter's face was grim as he absently patted the listless, mutilated animal. 'The 'breed did this?'

'Uh-huh. Wasn't gonna let him bring his butchery in here to my place but figured if I had the bronc where I could reach it, I could at least give it some kinda treatment.'

'Looks pretty far gone. Those flanks're infected.'

'Never had no attention — except rippin'-up by them lousy spurs. Mister, you make yourself to home anywhere in my stables. Damn, I can even clear a free area in the tack room if you prefer to spread your roll in more comfort . . . ?'

Hunter held up a hand. 'A corner of my own stall will do fine, friend.'

'An' breakfast on me!'

Hunter smiled wearily. 'I'll settle for a cup of coffee and flapjacks.'

'You're on. Now, there's anythin' you want durin' the night, I got me a local kid that sleeps here an' he'll — '

'Mister, you keep on offering me this and that and it'll be daybreak before I hit the sack! An' I'm mighty tuckered.'

'Oh, yeah — need a nightcap?' He indicated the neck of a bottle poking above his trouser belt. 'Homemade lightnin'.'

Hunter shook his head and, after

41

seeing to water for his nearby mount, Hunter finally spread one of his thin blankets over a layer of straw and stretched out, tugging his hat down, and yawned long and luxuriously.

★ ★ ★

But his awakening from the shallow sleep was much more violent — and even as the first kick thudded into one hip as he lifted a protecting leg instinctively, he heard a rough voice say, 'Yeah, that's the sonuver! Right where she said!'

'One deputy too many! Wake up, you son of a bitch!'

By then Hunter was grunting in pain, arms crossing over his head, lower body twisting, trying to get his knees under him for a solid thrust upright. There were two of them at least: lots of scuffling of boots in the straw, gruntings with effort.

Blood was oozing from his nostrils and his mouth was numb, which he figured meant a smashed lip. His head buzzed as knuckles like horseshoes slammed into the side of his neck. He fell against the wall — he had been half-rising, but now went down again, sliding to one knee first, then stumbling all the way.

Boots, knees, elbows, all drove home in jarring bursts of pain. He reared back to one knee, saw he was almost level with the lower belly of a man with torn corduroys, legs spread for purchase.

Hunter clawed his hand and drove it up violently deep into the crotch, closing his grip and twisting. There was a strangled scream and someone jumped away as the injured man fell, retching, to his knees. Hunter swung a boot against the other man's head to make sure he was out of it, then went after the one still on his feet.

But he'd miscounted: a thick body stepped out of the shadows and head-butted Hunter. He went down, groaning, lights streaking behind his rolling eyes. Something hit him so hard in the ribs he thought at first his own horse had stomped on him.

And then, as he tumbled into the yawning blackness, he recognized the livery man's voice.

'Get the hell outa here, you yaller bastards! Go on! I'll even risk shootin' one of my own broncs if you don't vamoose — and pronto!' Gun hammers clicked ominously.

Although the sub-conscious Hunter didn't see it, a band of light streaked across the metal of a sawn-off shotgun as the irate livery man brought up his weapon.

The attackers stumbled against each other, clawing wildly in desperate efforts to get out into the aisle and run for the big, open rear door of the stables.

★ ★ ★

The livery owner, Lester, came into the stall slopping soapy water from a battered tin dish, old rags stuffed into

44

his belt. He stopped in his tracks when he saw Sheriff McAdam standing beside a couple of hay bales that had been pushed together so Hunter could stretch out on them.

'The hell'd you come from, Mac?'

'Till I get some deputies, I do my own night patrols. There was enough racket here to make me think about callin' a damn posse!' The lawman's face was rawboned, eyes narrowed in anger, an accusation in his voice.

'Judas, I come down soon's I heard Ollie's voice and then the beatin' started!' Lester glanced at the bloody Hunter. 'Recognized Ollie, an' thought he'd be gunwhippin' this ranny like he usually does, the coyote. Hey, I din't waste no time, did I, pard?'

'You did OK, friend,' Hunter slurred, squeezing out the sodden rag with which he had been tenderly mopping his battered face. That satisfied McAdam, but there was suspicion in his voice as Lester worked over the quietly cursing Hunter.

'Seems they knew just where to come.'

Hunter glared out of one puffy eye. His swollen, split lips tightened painfully, oozing blood. 'They knew exactly where to find me.' He shook his head at McAdam. 'No, Lester didn't tell 'em, but I know who did!'

'Easy.' The lawman pressed a hand against Hunter's shoulder as the man started to rise. 'How d'you know?'

Hunter snorted, spat some blood. 'Well, one of 'em said 'He's right where she said he'd be'. You got any notion what — or who — he might've been talkin' about?'

The sheriff shook his head, frowning. 'No, Tess wouldn't do that! She wouldn't set Ollie and his drunken pards on you. She ain't that vindictive.'

'For Chris'sake! She still thinks I murdered her brothers two years ago! She practically kicked me out of her rooming-house and knew where I was aiming to sleep!'

'It ain't the kinda thing Tess Deacon

would do!' McAdam's voice was emphatic, his eyes cold and challenging.

Hunter took a fresh wet cloth Lester handed him and patted his battered face. He said, 'Why don't you go ask her?'

'By damn, I will! No! — You stay put. I'll bring you her answer, whatever it is.'

* * *

The girl was angry at being awakened and clutched the neck of the gown she had thrown over her night-dress firmly as she listened to Sheriff McAdam.

'That's what Ollie said, Tess. Lester heard it, clear as a bell. 'He's right where she said he'd be'. You gotta admit it sounds like you sent 'em after Hunter.'

'I never said any such thing . . . ' Her words trailed off and he was sure some blood drained from her face as she pushed hair back from her forehead, suddenly uncertain.

'Sure . . . ?' prompted the lawman.

A moment's silence and then she told him in a quiet, clear voice, 'Ollie came here after you and Hunter left. Said he'd decided to take the deputy's job and wanted to move into the room I was supposed to set aside. I told him that he wasn't staying under my roof for any reason and to get off my doorstoop.' She paused and briefly cleared her throat. 'I believe I said something like 'Go and do like Hunter has — go sleep with your horse — if it can stand your stench!' He reeked of booze, as usual of course.' She jerked her head, jaw thrusting defiantly. 'That's what I said, Foster, or very close to it. My God! What kind of person d'you think I am that I'd send Ollie and his drunken friends to beat up anyone!'

McAdam tugged lightly at his ear lobe. 'Well, Hunter ain't just *anyone* to you, Tess.'

He saw her rage instantly rise as she grabbed the edge of the door and slammed it in his face. Her trembling voice reached him through the quivering timber.

'If you value your life, Foster McAdam, you'd better not eat in my dining-room!'

Hunter, despite the hurt it caused him, grinned when the lawman reported back to the stables. Hunter had cleaned himself up some by now, though his face was, of course, still swollen, cut and bruised.

'You can tell her I believe her, Sheriff. I'm kinda glad, though, it was all a misunderstanding.'

'You tell her! I ain't goin' back there.'

'We-ell, mebbe we'll just let it slide and be done with it. By the way, I've decided I will take the deputy's job — looks like I'm gonna owe the sawbones, though.' He touched one deep bleeding cut on his cheek, another over his left eye. 'Might need an advance.'

McAdam smiled thinly. 'Job's yours. But Will Bardon is still going to want Ollie Revell for second man.'

Hunter smiled carefully with his puffed, twisted lips. 'Me, too.'

* ★ ★

'Sonuver did pretty damn good, seein' as there was three of us.' Ollie Revell worked cautiously at a loosened tooth. 'Woulda liked a little longer to give him a real gunwhippin' though.'

His two companions were Ollie's regular drinking pards, Stinger and Mitch. They now leaned against the rear of the saloon, passing around the flat bottle of bourbon Mitch had stolen from behind the bar while Ollie argued with the saloon man over some trivial matter until the man had called in the barrel-chested bouncers — then Ollie and his friends had hurried towards the rear door . . . with their bottle.

'How's it feel to be a depitty, Mr Revell, suh?'

'Wait till I get into my room at Tess Deacon's and I'm here to tell you that I know that job's gonna suit me fine.'

They laughed and swigged from the bottle, Stinger rubbing his hand over the open neck but pausing as he lifted it towards his lips.

'Judas Priest!' he gasped, the other two snapping their heads around as if their necks would crack.

Then the bottle exploded against Stinger's mouth, shattering his front teeth, the raw liquor burning his eyes. He had enough breath left to scream but it was strangled as he tried to spit broken glass out of his bleeding mouth.

'What the hell!' gasped Mitch.

Hunter stepped around the framework at the bottom of the saloon steps, casually grabbed Stinger by the neck, the groaning man now doubled over, and drove him face first into the post. Mitch recovered before Ollie and jumped in, dragging his gun free of leather.

It whistled past Hunter's head as he ducked and came up inside Mitch's swing. He hooked an elbow into the man's ribs and Mitch sank to his knees, groaning. Hunter's knee took him under the jaw and stretched him out on the ground with the accumulated rubbish.

Ollie Revell was alert now and jumped at Hunter, catching him a blow on the side of the neck.

'You damn well a glutton for punishment ain't you!' Ollie panted, driving a hammer blow at Hunter's head.

But the down-driving fist was caught in something like the jaws of a vice and twisted painfully, bringing Ollie to his toes, sobbing in pain. He yelled as he felt a tendon tear, then he was forced back against the wall, held there by Hunter's body.

'Heard you like to work folk over with a gun barrel, Ollie.' Hunter's voice was like a snake's hiss as he forced the words into Revell's ear. 'But you dunno what a real gunwhippin's like. Was a place in Mexico I was in once and there was a guard there — here, lemme show you.'

Ollie started forward with a lurch as Hunter's pressure eased some and then his head slammed back against the woodwork. Lights swirled behind his eyes — but he could see the blued-steel barrel of Hunter's sixgun, only inches from his face. 'Trick is to be — quick!'

The barrel blurred back and forth across Ollie's jolting face as Hunter's hand moved. Metal tore skin and blood sprayed, Ollie's nose broke and he almost choked on his own blood as he tried to yell. In seconds his face was a red network of streaks of blood, drooling. Ollie's knees sagged.

Hunter twisted his fingers in the sweaty hair, turned the gun sideways so the blade foresight was against Revell's already lacerated skin. The whites of Ollie's eyes showed plainly and Hunter suddenly eased the pressure. Instead, he sharply rapped the bridge of the already busted nose and Ollie Revell went down all the way, spreading out in the dust, writhing as he moaned.

He was alone in his misery, his pards

having faded quickly into the night.

Hunter turned fast, the gun spinning in his grip, hammer cocking under his thumb as he automatically went into a gunfighter's crouch.

He recognized Foster McAdam's silhouette against the dim street light, gently eased down the hammer spur on his Colt as light blazed briefly from the sheriff's weapon.

McAdam used a boot to turn the groaning Ollie on to his back.

'When Will Bardon hears about this, could be you'll have already lost that deputy's job before you even got started.'

'Thought I was already doin' the job.' Hunter gestured to the moaning, bleeding trio. 'These're the three *hombres* jumped me in the livery — Lester'll back me on that. Figured you wouldn't want scum like this roamin' the streets scarin' the citizens.'

'You didn't recognize 'em right away huh? Even though I'd pointed them out to you, *named* Ollie as a prospective deputy?'

Hunter leaned forward stiffly because of some of the bandages the doctor had used on his injuries. 'So that's Ollie Revell? He has a lot to learn about a real gunwhippin'.'

'I think he knows now. He was to be your 'deputy-deputy' — you like to put it that way.'

'He'll recover — his kind always do.'

''Specially when their brother-in-law's head of the town council! You damn idiot! You just might've gun-whipped your way out of the chief deputy's job.'

'Goddamn!' Hunter swore, then looked levelly into the lawman's face. 'Reckon it might've been worth it.'

As they walked away from the small crowd that had gathered, men grinning at the sight of Ollie's battered figure, McAdam murmured, 'You could be right.'

5

Mystery Man

Now it was Foster McAdam's job to notify Will Bardon of his brother-in-law's fate and the sheriff wasn't looking forward to doing it.

Ollie Revell was a sadistic bully and had been long overdue for the kind of thrashing Hunter had dealt out to him. Even Will Bardon knew that but, of course, had to turn a jaundiced eye, seeing as he was backing Ollie for the deputy's job . . . and married to Ollie's elder sister, Thora.

Bardon was a haughty man, not pleased to be dragged from the arms of a warm and exciting woman (not his bona fide wife) to be faced with the news that Revell had been gunwhipped stupid by this newcomer, Hunter.

Tall, well-built, Bardon favoured a

bushy, though carefully trimmed moustache. Hard eyes stared at the lawman in the lamplight of Bardon's office and he tugged his silk gown across his sweating chest saying, 'It would take a good man to beat Ollie at gunwhipping,' he said quietly.

It was the last kind of remark that McAdam expected and he just stopped his jaw dropping open in time, frowned slightly as he watched the other man. *What happened to the expected outrage? 'My brother-in-law attacked? By God! Who dared do it . . . ?'* But something had thrown Bardon on to another tack . . .

'Well, that's right, Will. A good, tough man. But are there enough folk in town to agree with that and still have this Hunter for my chief deputy? I mean, he's shown how hard he can be and I've seen how brutal he is when he's riled — just ask Ollie and the two men he put in Doc Earls' infirmary.'

Bardon pursed his lips, almost absently ran a thumbnail over the moustache. 'You know anything about him?'

Again, McAdam answered slowly — this was not taking the direction he had expected — and, what's more, he could not quite see where it was going. Not on Bardon's past performances ... *tantrums* better described some of the man's rages when something went awry with his plans.

'Not much, Will. He was a trick-shooter with a travellin' show, but he's also a real-life gunfighter. He says he tracked that 'breed for three years. So, if he sets out to do a job, he'll see it all the way through no matter how long it takes. These things are obvious enough, but I dunno much more — No, wait! He told me he had some trouble down in Mexico after the war. But what *gringo* didn't at that time? Can't find any wanted dodger on him ... '

McAdam's voice trailed off slowly as Bardon's mouth moved in a slow smile, stretching the moustache. He snapped his fingers.

'The name rang a bell! Yes: *Hunter*! What kind of trouble was it in Mexico?'

McAdam's frown deepened at Bardon's interest. 'Some hoo-rawin' thing that got outa hand. You know: a bunch of Reb survivors on the run at that time, kickin' over the traces, livin' by their wits. Damn Yankees wanted to keep 'em south of the Rio where they wouldn't cause problems to the New Union they were tryin' to build . . . He mighta been runnin' a few guns to the Mex rebels, too, but I'd say there was no politics involved — just makin' a fast buck.'

'Politics!' cut in Bardon. 'Wait a minute — he was mixed up in politics down there, wasn't he?'

'Hell, Will, I don't know anythin' about that except he got caught up with a bunch who went off the rails and one tried to assassinate some Mex official for the hell of it . . . what difference does it make now?'

'Probably none,' Bardon said a mite distractedly.

McAdam was disconcerted by the man's strange attitude. *This was the last reaction the sheriff had expected from a man whose stated intention was to run this town his way. Yet, his own brother-in-law had been beaten to a jelly and he hadn't even made a decent protest yet.*

Suddenly, Bardon's face sobered. 'Damn gunfighters think they can come into anybody's town and run loose! But, at the same time, we need a tough man to give you the backing you'll require, Foster. Once those trail herds start coming through, this is going to be one wild place, and you have to admit you're gettin' on apiece.'

'Only four-and-a-half years older'n you, Will!'

Bardon smiled thinly. 'A man can cram a lot of living — and knowledge — in that time, Foster. But, while I'm sorry for Ollie' — he paused and gave an unconvincing grimace as he shrugged his wide shoulders — 'and no doubt my wife will kick up a fuss, I think a man like Hunter is *just* what we need here.'

McAdam was stunned, but, at the same time elated. *His job would be a damn sight easier with a man of Hunter's talents and reputation at his side.*

He just wished like hell he savvied why Will Bardon wanted to hire the man who had half-killed his wife's brother. Especially when everyone in town knew that Thora Revell Bardon had as mean a streak as Ollie did running through her corsetted, coiffured and pampered body.

But not everyone knew just how much Will Bardon was prepared to put up with — as long as his wife's legacy from her previous marriage was still within his grasp. It was, of course, at a time when a woman had very few, if any, rights. She virtually owned nothing: whatever she brought with her to a marriage became her husband's the moment she said 'I do'.

Although, there *could* be contrived

delays — as Bardon was finding out right now — but in the long run, he would have what he wanted. Under his guidance, Cimarron Valley — or Springs or Flats, whatever the name — could eventually lead to political leadership of an entirely new county that he envisaged — a long way off yet, but in Bardon's manipulating hands it would soon enough be appearing on the maps.

★   ★   ★

Hunter was as surprised as McAdam when the sheriff gave him the news that Bardon seemed happy enough to have the gunfighter wear the chief deputy's badge.

He shook hands perfunctorily with the sheriff, looking into the man's eyes. 'You told Ollie yet?' he asked wryly.

'Leaving that to Will.'

'How much trouble can I expect from Ollie?'

McAdam bored a finger absently into

one ear. 'About as much as possible. You not only whipped him, you did it in front of his cronies, and now, any backing he'd hoped to get from his brother-in-law simply isn't there . . . I'd say Ollie's not a happy man — and likely won't be — until he sees you dead.'

Hunter nodded as if this was about what he had expected, adding, 'How about this sister?'

McAdam shrugged. 'Their marriage has been a long on-off battle over one thing or another. Neither'll give in to the other. Will's bound to pay in some way, but in the end he'll still have *his* way.'

Hunter looked at the used but still shiny deputy's badge McAdam had given him. 'First time I've ever had anythin' like this to back up my gun.'

'We'll give you the oath and get you settled in proper accommodation.'

The sheriff smiled slowly as Hunter's face straightened.

'Yeah,' was the new deputy's only comment.

★ ★ ★

'I will not have the man who murdered my brothers living under my roof!' Tess Deacon stamped her foot so hard for emphasis that the twinge of pain it caused in her left knee made her wince.

Will Bardon, dressed in his sharp, grey-striped business suit, ready for yet another day's work that would put him closer to his goal, removed his bowler hat — imported from Boston, specially for him — and fanned his sweating face briefly: summer was bringing its heat early this year.

He was standing on the stoop of Tess's side entrance and now smiled without any trace of humour, although his moustache did seem to twitch a little.

'Well, now, Tess, Foster has told me about your bias and I hasten to add that I completely understand your attitude.'

He swiftly held up a hand as she started to speak. 'During our various enquiries, the council learned about your freight bill with Hasluck's — now hear me out! and, as you are one of the original citizens in our community, we decided to award you the accommodation allowance. We thought it would help you out, settling Hasluck's bill, and give you a less stressful time of it. You realize, of course, we are all in for some changes once we declare ourselves a trail town.'

Tess's face was pale and tight, and he could hear the breath hissing through that small nose.

'We are all aware of some . . . wilder times to come, Will, and I'm grateful to council for considering me, but — '

She stopped as he held up a hand.

'Allow me to elaborate upon that 'but' — such a small word with a huge potential for good — or bad.'

She was trembling a little now as she began to realize what Bardon was about to say.

And he said it — almost word for word what she had only this instant imagined in her mind.

'You see, Hasluck realizes there is a huge potential in his business once we're a full-blown trail town and he wants all his outstanding accounts taken care of before he makes his approaches to his own suppliers. He'll need a good deal of credit to expand of course — '

'You are a devious swine, aren't you, Will?'

'I — er — would hardly put it quite like that!' he snapped.

'Then spell it out: my freight bill with Hasluck will be — 'taken care of' — provided I allow this new *deputy* to live here.'

'Well, it'll be to your advantage, Tess. No bills, just incoming room and board.'

'You know damn well I have to give in, don't you?'

He smiled, then nodded almost imperceptibly as he reached to an inside pocket and drew out a set of slim papers tied with a pink ribbon. 'It's all set out here, Tess, totally legal, prepared by my most experienced clerk, and — '

Tess suddenly stood to one side, her lips stretched so tightly they were almost white. 'Then let us get the damn formalities over and done with as quickly as possible.'

Some minutes later when she was signing the heavy legal paper where he indicated, his manicured fingernail tapping impatiently, she hesitated with her pen poised, looked up into Bardon's face, causing him to give a small jerk of surprise at the contempt in her eyes.

'I was just wondering, Will, why is it so important for you to have this . . . killer, living under my roof?'

'Oh, I wouldn't be too hard on him, Tess. He is just the kind of man we're going to need here, like it or not.'

Soberly, she nodded. 'Unfortunately that seems to be true. But I sense something different here, with this mystery man, Hunter. I believe you want him where you can find him quickly and call — '

He flipped open the gold pocket watch he suddenly produced from his suede vest. 'Would you mind just signing, Tess? I have other important appointments to keep and — '

As she scrawled her signature, she knew she was right: Bardon, for some reason, needed this Hunter where he could be found in a hurry.

She wondered what the reason could be: a sly, ambitious and ruthless man like Will Bardon, needing the services of a — let's face it! — the services of a cold-blooded killer.

She wondered just what kind of town Cimarron Springs was really going to be.

6

The Room

He smelled the room before he reached the end of the upstairs passage. A pleasant, disinfectant smell, and he was just in time to see the Indian maid with her bucket and mop, turn to close the door.

'Hey!'

The maid turned her head sharply, the hard-etched planes of her face showing she was a full-blood. She stared. He gestured to the room and his gear that he was carrying.

'I'll move in now,' he said evenly, not smiling because experience had shown him a smile never went anywhere with full-bloods addressed by whites.

She must have turned the handle, for the door swung open and she pushed past him, head down, a fistful of muddy water slopping out of the bucket on to one of his dusty boots. It might have been deliberate, though he didn't think so, and pretended he didn't notice. The maid lurched away to the stairs and started down as he went into the room and closed the door behind him.

He slung his blanket roll and saddle-bags on to the freshly made bed, seeing one frayed corner of the maroon cover, sat down on it, testing the mattress, then swung up his long legs.

As he did, the door opened and Tess Deacon stood there, unsmiling. 'At least you took your spurs off first, but don't make a habit of lying there with your boots on.'

Hunter swung his legs to the floor and stood up, a little surprised to find that close up, she wasn't quite as tall as he had figured. 'It'll do. Do I have a view?'

As he spoke he went to the balcony doors, opened them and stepped out on to a small platform.

His eyes opened wide. From street

level and inside the building, he hadn't any idea of the rooming-house's position in the town. Now he saw that it angled across the wide street and actually faced down a continuation of that street towards Main.

There he saw the saloon and another building across a narrow alley from it, which had a railed-in balcony on what must be the roof of the offices beneath. It immediately made him think of a speaking platform and he turned to ask Tess. But she was ahead of him, had seen what he was trying to figure out.

'That's the Cimarron County Building. Just a small collection of offices at present but Will Bardon has bigger and better plans, he claims, for it. It replaces a lawyer's offices that were burned down.'

'Handy if he gets thirsty,' he said, with a jerk of his head toward the saloon, hoping to lighten the scene, but Tess remained sober.

'I wouldn't know. I have as little as possible to do with the council — and

71

Will Bardon in particular.'

'But you're still landed with me.'

Their gazes locked and she drew herself up a little. 'That is my misfortune. If there's anything you need, tug that rope in the corner: one of the maids or roustabouts will come up.'

She turned away but he reached out quickly to touch her arm, saw the flare behind her eyes in time and let his hand drop to his side. 'Listen, I'm gonna be here for a spell. Is this how it's gonna be, between you and me?'

'Yes. I keep a clean establishment and I expect my tenants to do their bit in keeping their room from looking like a pigsty. There's a notice that tells you the time of your meals and if you are not here for them . . . ' She shrugged her shoulders. 'That's your bad luck. There are no second sittings.'

She turned and left him staring at the inside of the door she closed behind her.

He rolled a cigarette and got it burning, leaned against the small balcony's rail as he smoked. *She sure was unbending, but hell, he likely wouldn't see much of her anyway, what with different shifts and night patrols.*

He flicked the cigarette down into the empty street below when he had smoked enough and hitched automatically at his gunbelt, looking about him as he did so. It was afternoon and there was an almost golden glow beginning to bathe the town. There was a little more noise from the saloon now as the afternoon drinking slid into the more serious night-time sessions. Turning away to start his unpacking — meagre though it was — he suddenly stopped.

The slanting sun was throwing the shadows of the rooming-house and other nearby buildings on clapboard walls and the dusty street itself. As Hunter moved, he caught a glimpse of his own shadow on the balcony.

But there was something else: the outline of the roof of Tess's place above where he stood was clear to see and Hunter frowned. There was something wrong here ... a sudden lift to the roof-line, almost as if there was another cubicle-sized room directly above where he was standing.

Leaning far out and turning awkwardly so his back was mostly resting on the rails, he saw there was something up there. Precariously, he balanced on the rails, pulling himself up by the overhang and found himself looking at a narrow, clapboard, cubicle-like structure, not much bigger than a large coffin. With imagination it could even be described as a small tower — *very* small.

'Now what the *hell* is that doing there? And what *is* the damn thing?'

★   ★   ★

He waited until the evening meal was over — good grub, too: roast beef that didn't bend your teeth, flavoured with spices that didn't dissolve a man's tonsils, and plenty of fresh vegetables. There was some custard thing for

74

dessert which was OK, but sweet, sloppy dishes weren't much to Hunter's taste.

He was smoking in his chair, alone at the table now, as the maids worked taking away the used dishes. Then Tess Deacon came in to inspect the progress and stopped in her tracks.

'We do have a smoking room,' she told him in her usual clipped tones, gesturing through a doorway.

'Yeah, saw the sign. Do you smoke?'

She blinked. 'I do not!'

'Figured that, so reckoned if I wanted to talk to you, I'd best wait in here.'

She turned and snapped some orders at a couple of giggling town girls who were obviously trying to earn a few extra cents for themselves by helping out. As they hurried to obey, Tess turned her unsmiling face to Hunter.

'I can't think of anything we need to say to one another.'

He let her start to turn and walk away, then said, 'All I want to know is what the hell's that thing on the roof

75

above my balcony.'

Tess paused abruptly, a frown creasing her smooth forehead. For a moment there he thought her eyes looked uncomfortable, then she said, 'It's an old construction left-over from Rosa's days. It has nothing to do with your room or, indeed, the main building, just something that was never demolished.'

'Well, what is it? Was it?'

Tess made an exasperated motion. 'Look, this is a very busy time for me — I can't explain and — believe me, it has nothing to do with your room or anyone else's. In fact, I'd almost forgotten the darn thing was there.'

'This Rosa sounds as if she was a bit of a crack-brain . . . '

'Rosa was . . . eccentric. She enjoyed life in . . . well, lots of ways no one else would. But she's long gone and I'd be obliged if you were the same — I *do* have a lot of work to do.'

He stood. 'Nice meal, ma'am,' he said and walked through the door leading to the smoking room.

She stood there, still frowning slightly, staring after him, and then her mouth tightened.

Of all the things for him to notice — that *thing* on the roof!

And she felt that Hunter was just the type to poke about until his curiosity was satisfied.

*   *   *

'You mean that little tower thing up there?' Sheriff Foster McAdam drew the brass-bristle brush carefully through the long bore of his Winchester, sighted down the rifling and picked up an oily rag to rub over the rifle's action.

'Got my curiosity,' Hunter told him, sitting across from the sheriff's desk.

'You can't see it from here.'

'Angle of the roofs block it, I guess, but it looks down towards Main and the county building according to Tess Deacon.'

McAdam's gaze sharpened. 'You gettin' along?'

'A long way apart — no matter. But this roof thing . . . '

McAdam went on cleaning and assembling his rifle as he spoke.

'One of Rosa's crazy ideas. She had a reputation for makin' pigeon pie flavoured with her special sauce — which seemed to be mostly tequila.'

Hunter grimaced a little and McAdam smiled. 'You'd be surprised how popular it was. Anyway, the best pigeons used the roof of the bank until they built the county offices. 'Till then she used to potshot the birds from her kitchen stoop with a little .22 calibre carbine, but when the birds moved they used the roof of the saloon. She couldn't get a clear shot, ripped off some shingles and got into a hassle with the saloon crowd and Will Bardon, who was just fitting out an office for himself in the new county building. Next thing, she's built this privy on her roof — it's not a privy but everyone calls it that. She had a good view up there and got all the birds she wanted — until a ricochet sent a splinter into the eye of Lance McGill, Bardon's head clerk, so she switched to a slingshot. Damn good with it too.'

Hunter smiled. 'She sounds like one wild woman, this Rosa.'

'She livened up the town. But that's how come that privy thing is there. I guess Tess cut it off from the main rooming-house. Be full of cobwebs and rats now.'

'Heard somethin' scuttling around.' Hunter stood, hitching at his gunbelt as he glanced at the wall clock. 'About time for me to start night patrol.'

McAdam looked surprised, still wiping down his rifle. 'Didn't realize. Look it's early, still dusk — I usually have my supper first. You come on home and meet the wife. No, no, don't worry: she always makes plenty to go around. We'll have supper, then I'll show you my routine. Feel free to change it any way you like — OK?'

'See I'm gonna put on weight in this job.'

7

Night Stalk

There wasn't a lot to Cimarron Springs — as yet. But Hunter knew — from McAdam constantly telling him — that once the big herds rolled in from the outlying counties and some of the distant spreads pushing back into the ranges got to hear, that there was now an easy pass to the railroad.

'Fireworks,' McAdam said at the end of his long dissertation. 'She'll light up like the Fourth of July and stay that way for the whole blamed season.'

'We're gonna be busy then.'

The sheriff smiled at Hunter's dry comment. 'You could say that. Now, you OK to find your way around to the edge of town and work that circuit I use? You might come up with one you like better but stay with mine for now and if you figure different we'll check it out in daylight first.'

As the sheriff turned away, he called back softly over his shoulder, 'Doc Earls tells me Ollie Revell kicked up a storm at his infirmary and dragged Stinger and Mitch O'Day outa their sick beds.' Hunter remained silent. 'You know what I'm sayin'?'

'Sure. I'll play the Good Samaritan if I run into 'em — and see they get their proper rest.'

He heard the lawman chuckle as he walked away without looking back.

* * *

Hunter took it slow, even paused to allow the barkeep to buy him a beer in the big smoky saloon, the walls still bullet-pocked from the recent fracas.

'Seen the O'Days?' he asked casually.

The 'keep paused, wiping out a glass with a none-too-clean cloth. 'Stinger an' Mitch you mean?'

'Sounds right.'

The barman licked his lips. 'No, I ain't seen 'em.' Then he lowered his voice and added, 'Nor will you — if they're out on the hunt. Got a name for bein' mighty good stalkers, know what I mean?'

Hunter set down his empty glass, adjusted his hat and started for the side door. 'Think I'll go look.'

'Er — Rear door's a shortcut to Hammerhead Alley. Just make sure you turn left. Mighty dark t'other way.'

The deputy nodded soberly and changed direction to the rear door, a couple of drinkers quickly moving aside.

It was dark and cool outside and he stepped to the hinged side of the door as it swung closed, cutting a few moments off the time he was outlined by the bar's lights. Then he moved left quickly, crouching, his Colt sliding into his hand. He had kept his eyes squinted but it was still too dark for him to make out shapes — except for the angular ends of old crates casually tossed there by the saloon.

Even as he swept his narrowed gaze along the crates' outline, a sharp angle near the right end suddenly took on a smoother, rounder look as if something up there moved.

There was also a faint, barely distinctive blur beneath that changing shape.

Maybe from bandages around a man's head?

He shouldn't have paused to get the possible explanation clear in his head. Suddenly the alley's dark night flared with the thundering roar of a shotgun and Hunter felt the searing punch of buckshot across his shoulders. His hat spun away and he dropped instinctively as the second barrel of the shotgun — *behind* him and not from the place he had been looking! — filled the alley with its blast.

A set-up! And he'd walked right into it.

He was already moving and thrust with his boots now, stretching his long body out as he hurtled forward. He felt his shirt flapping around his back and a spreading wet heat high on his shoulder that set him stumbling.

His body smashed at least two crates and a sixgun triggered three fast shots in his direction. Hunter was acting by pure instinct now, rolled on to his side, kicked away from a pile of splintered crates that fell with a clatter. He thought he heard a man curse but then came the unmistakable sound of a shotgun's breech closing on a fresh load with a chilling, metallic *clack*!

He got his boots against something solid and snapped his legs straight, using his free left hand to push off from the ground. He almost did a back somersault, his feet going higher than his head. Then he was rolling with crates spilling around him. The sixgun was barking, someone was yelling, and another voice cursed a used shell that had jammed only halfway out of the breech.

Hunter slammed broken crates aside, saw the now unmistakable bandaged head of Mitch O'Day as the man roared a stream of bad language, wading through the debris, smoking Colt rising, then throwing down as he spotted Hunter's writhing body.

The deputy worked his shoulders so as to give himself enough freedom to chop at his Colt's hammer with the edge of his left hand. Three rapid shots and Mitch lifted to his toes, a scream cut off by a sudden, bubbling, choking sound from his bullet-torn throat.

Hunter rolled away as Mitch spilled forward, a corpse already, before hitting the pile of splintered wood.

Then Stinger roared a foul curse and came wading in, swinging the shotgun by the hot barrels, the used shell presumably still jammed in the breech.

He was mouthing unintelligible curses, spittle flying, his own bandages showing as a pale blur each time he swung the gun, missing Hunter by inches.

The deputy twisted on to hands and knees, jerked his head aside as the butt of the Greener slammed past close enough to sweep his hair across his forehead. Maniacally, eyes staring like the whites of boiled eggs in his crazy face, Stinger reared above Hunter, shotgun raised high over his head, barrels gripped in both hands.

The blow, if delivered, would have crushed Hunter's skull — but it never reached him.

He stretched up as high as he could, felt his Colt's muzzle dig deeply into Stinger's belly, or that soft spot just at the arch of the ribs. Hoping there was still a cartridge under the hammer, he fired. There was a muffled sound and the gun almost twisted from his grip with recoil as warm blood spurted over his hand.

Stinger O'Day let out a long, gusting sigh and his jerking body collapsed, the empty shotgun falling with a clatter . . .

Hunter was leaning against the saloon wall, reloading, when gawkers spilled out of the doorway and gathered round. Sheriff McAdam lumbered up, panting, gun ready in his hand.

Someone waved a lantern around, the light reflecting redly from the blood-spattered alley.

A man was violently sick as McAdam used his rifle muzzle to roll over Mitch O'Day. He turned a sober face towards Hunter.

'I gotta tell you, not all night patrols are like this.'

'For which I'm truly thankful. They didn't waste any time. I'd barely started my rounds.'

McAdam nodded soberly. 'Shouldn't've sent you on my usual route — ought've given you a new one. Still, we got two less hardcases to bother us now.' The sheriff looked around at the jostling men.

'Someone's mighty trigger-happy, you ask me,' a man growled.

'Step into that dark alley, friend,' Hunter invited quietly. 'I'll come in soon and I'll cock my gun when I do. Tell me what your reaction is.'

There was murmuring and the man who had made the remark said, 'OK. I guess I'd've started shootin', too. You gonna notch your guns? I mean, three dead men in three days!'

'I'll pass on the notchin',' Hunter told him. 'But I don't mind if you keep the hardcases comin'.'

'Judas! What kinda man'd say that?' a raspy voice queried.

'Someone who's hell in a hand basket,' another allowed.

'If he means it,' a third man said sceptically, keeping well back in the crowd.

'He does,' the sheriff said, stepping forward. 'Now let's get this mess cleaned up.'

★ ★ ★

Once again, McAdam was surprised at Will Bardon's reaction when he was told about the gunfight behind the saloon.

'Well, it doesn't surprise me that mean-assed men like the O'Days tried to even the score, Foster.'

'No-ooo. But the whole town's already talkin' about the way Hunter took 'em on — with some buckshot wounds in his back, too! Killed 'em both,' the sheriff replied quietly.

Bardon turned to him and lit a short cigar, the flaring light briefly showing his smile.

'Doing the job he's being paid for — that's the kind of deputy we need, Foster. Someone to make the wild boys think twice before they take on our Hunter.'

Our Hunter!

McAdam was stunned. 'I'm glad he's on our side, Will, but — well as someone pointed out, he's only just arrived and has already killed three men.'

Bardon blew smoke across McAdam's seamed face. 'Yeah, he's a killer, all right.'

Well, what the hell makes you sound so damn pleased about that? the sheriff thought as Bardon abruptly walked off with a couple of his local businessmen cronies.

It seemed that Stinger had been trying to blow Hunter's head off with the shotgun, so he had fired at an upward angle. But, cramped by the stack of crates, it was too steep, too far left, and only a few of the buckshot in the deadly pattern touched the deputy.

His left shoulder was going to be stiff and possibly the inner edge of his right shoulder blade. A small notch had been cut from his left ear but stopped bleeding when the sawbones dabbed some kind of balsam over it. The wound stung like hell and Hunter let the doctor know it in colourful language.

'Looking at the scars on your body, I'd say that would be classed as a minor wound for a man like you, Deputy.'

Hunter said nothing and the old doctor's wrinkles moved a shade around his mouth. 'I'd think you ought to be used to this kind of thing.'

'Then you oughta know better, Doc. I'd rather get along without any wounds, minor or otherwise.'

'You don't seem to be trying very hard,' the medic said, a mite peeved. 'Three men dead since you arrived in town.'

'How you prefer men like that, Doc? Walkin' around doin' their mischief, or six feet under, talking to the earthworms?'

The medic went on about his work in silence and when he had finished, said, 'Perhaps you could be an asset to this town after all, or the town it's shaping up to be.'

'How much I owe you, Doc?'

'I . . . think . . . nothing for this time. I'll take a gamble and hope the next time you won't need my attentions in my other capacity.'

Hunter frowned, shrugging into his ruined shirt. The doctor smiled thinly and pointed to a sign on the wall.

'Just don't go arrangin' anythin' for me without my permission, Doc,' Hunter said as he left.

He heard the sawbones chuckling

even after he'd closed the infirmary door.

★ ★ ★

To add to McAdam's puzzlement over Bardon so readily accepting Hunter's violent tendencies, the councillor told him, 'We'll buy you a new shirt, Deputy. I believe it would be an acceptable expense in your work.'

Hunter seemed somewhat surprised, too, but nodded his thanks.

'You can take him down to my store, Foster.'

Outside the council offices, Hunter commented, 'Our friend Bardon seems to have a lot invested in this town, or what he hopes to make it.'

The sheriff nodded, seeming only vaguely interested. But a few paces on, after they had crossed the street to the painted façade of Bardon's Ladies' and Gents' Outfitters, he said, 'It seems to me Will Bardon and his cronies have been making plans for this place a lot longer than anyone realized — leastways, that *I* knew. Guess he'd figure I'd just go along with whatever he wanted, anyway.'

Hunter glanced at him sharply as they entered the store. 'Would you?'

'Man my age, married, job prospects lookin' more or less permanent? Be a fool not to — also, not much choice.'

'There's always a choice,' Hunter said shortly, as he started looking at some plain blue and grey shirts.

McAdam flushed slightly. 'And the gun was yours?'

Hunter flicked his gaze at him briefly. 'Sometimes the 'choice' is forced on you.'

McAdam smiled thinly. 'By the way, Doc said you'd better take a day or two off till those buckshot wounds heal a little more. He reckons your shoulder muscles could cramp if you have to use your gun in a hurry.'

'That's the usual way.'

The sheriff paused. 'You're not going to take time off?'

'Sure — see if I can find Ollie Revell.'

'Dammit, Hunter! Do you *like* trouble?'

'Love it — and like to square it away soon as I can.'

'You'll never prove that Ollie turned those O'Days loose just to ambush you.'

'I don't need to prove it — that's what he did.'

'I guess I agree, but, we're s'posed to be *lawmen* which means we have to go by the book.'

'Mostly, I want to find out who put him up to it.'

The sheriff's frown deepened and he waved away the clerk impatiently. But Hunter gave a nod and the man took the shirts away to wrap.

'Ollie's not smart enough to know he's been used that way,' McAdam said quietly. Hunter nodded and waited till the clerk handed him the package and named the price. The deputy looked at the sheriff, raising his eyebrows quizzically.

'Council agreed to replace one shirt — you've ordered two.'

Hunter nodded, turned to the clerk. 'So I did, friend. Will Bardon is paying for one of those shirts, have I got enough credit here for the other one?'

The thin-faced clerk looked kind of shiftily at the carefully deadpanned sheriff, cleared his throat and said, 'I should think you do, Deputy, but mebbe I should check with the councillor . . . ?'

McAdam sighed, placing some coins on the counter. 'Don't bother, Kel. I see by the look on your face that Deputy Hunter's already impressed you. I'll OK it with Councillor Bardon.'

The man looked relieved and, as he started to go, Hunter said, 'That a tool rack I see along there?'

'Yessir. We supply most anything.'

'Might take a look before we go.'

Outside the store, McAdam said sourly, 'That clerk nearly fell over himself showin' you them hammers and chisels. Seems you've not only earned

Bardon's approval.'

'But not yours? You havin' second thoughts about giving me the job?'

'Mebbe, but mebbe not in the way you think. Look, Hunter, I-I dunno if you'll savvy what I'm going to say but — Will Bardon was all goody-goody about hiring a sidekick for me: had to be slick with a gun, of course, but also had to show a bit of caution where and how he used it. You were nowhere near the top of Bardon's list until — suddenly, you killed the 'breed, beat the daylights out of the O'Days and Ollie Revell — which should have lost you the job right away, by rights, Ollie being Will's brother-in-law. But seems to me, that impressed Will no end.'

'Mebbe he doesn't really like Ollie, brother-in-law or not.'

'Hell, he don't like him at all! But I ... I've thought a lot about this because it puzzles me. I reckon he was impressed with your ruthlessness, I guess I'd call it, but the kind a lawman has to use at times.'

'Well, what the hell're you saying? You've kind of lost me.'

McAdam sighed. 'Yeah, myself, too. But I came to the conclusion — and I still believe this — Will Bardon wants a real killer wearing a badge here, no matter what he says different. And I reckon you're honest enough to admit that you fit the bill perfectly.'

After a pause, Hunter asked quietly, 'For what exactly?'

'That's what I can't figure. Bardon's turned right around from only considering men with a good, law-abiding reputation as a deputy, to — well, practically openly endorsing a — a — '

'Cold-blooded killer,' Hunter finished for him. 'Yeah, I think I see what you mean now. The tag don't bother me any, but Bardon's reason for wanting someone like me on his payroll kinda makes me wonder.'

'*Now* you see my problem.'

Hunter turned his clear blue eyes towards the sheriff.

'Mebbe there ain't any problem.

Mebbe it's as simple as Bardon wanting someone dead somewhere down the line and now he figures he knows where he can find a man to do the job.'

McAdam stiffened. He started to speak, paused, and just then Lester appeared, leading a limping horse on its way to the blacksmith's forge at the end of the street.

'Lester, you seen Ollie Revell?' Hunter asked.

Lester paused and spat. 'Too many damn times! But if you mean recent, yeah. Picked up his mount and had a grubsack with him. Link, my stable-hand, says he was bitchin' about havin' to ride on an errand for Will Bardon that'd keep him away at least over-night.'

'That'd be Ollie,' McAdam opined, then said to Hunter, 'Will gettin' him outa town for a spell.'

Hunter nodded. 'He's gotta come back.'

The sheriff frowned slightly, exchanging a glance with Lester.

'Hell! Then I hope I see the sonuver one more time,' the liveryman said, 'when you go to meet him, Hunter.'

'Could be something to see,' McAdam opined slowly.

8

Downtime

At the corner of Main and Cedar Street, down which was Tess Deacon's rooming-house, the sheriff and Hunter paused, taking last drags on the cigarettes they had been smoking. Both flipped away the burning stubs at about the same time.

'You gonna take time off then?'

Hunter shrugged, winced as the shallow though tender wounds moved under the bandages. 'Might's well — town's gonna be pretty quiet for a day or two I reckon.'

McAdam smiled thinly. 'Could be right.' He hesitated, started to speak, then lifted a hand to his hat brim. 'Mebbe I'll drop in to your room when I'm doin' the rounds tonight.'

'Don't wake me if I don't answer

after the first knock.'

The sheriff smiled, turned away, but again paused.

Hunter frowned, puzzled. 'The hell's wrong with you, Mac? You got something you want to get off your chest?'

McAdam's lips tightened a little: he ought to have known Hunter would know what he had to ask.

'Well? Would you?'

'Would I what?' Hunter retorted carefully. 'You're gonna have to spell it out, Mac.'

McAdam sighed. 'OK, fair enough. You said back there that maybe Bardon wants someone killed later and he figures you'll be around to do it for him . . . *will* you?'

'Be around? Or will I do it?'

'You're an aggravatin' sonuver! You know damn well what I want to know!'

Hunter, deadpan, shrugged and, as McAdam's face started to darken, held up a hand quickly, almost dropping his parcel of shirts.

'Don't have a heart attack! Mac, you ain't known me long, but you're a pretty smart old coot — all right, all right, forget that 'old'. You told me once you prided yourself on being able to judge a man pretty good, so . . . what d'you think?'

'I think we're gonna find out in a couple minutes who draws fastest here! Goddamnit, Hunter! Gimme a straight answer!'

Hunter saw he had pushed the sheriff far enough, looked steadily into the seamed face. 'I don't do assassinations. I'll call a man out and square off, if I figure I have a reason. I'll hire out my gun in a range war or even bounty-huntin', if I'm desperate, but I won't hire out to go and kill a man just because someone asks me to or offers cold cash. Plain enough?'

'What I figured, but — '

'You had to hear me say it.'

'I'm like that.' McAdam paused, looked steadily into Hunter's face. 'And you did tell me you'd been kinda mixed up in some sort of assassination attempt in Mexico.'

Hunter dismissed that with a wave of his hand. 'We were just around to take the blame is all, but it blew over.'

'All proved innocent?'

Hunter frowned. 'Hell, we didn't stick around to find out one way or t'other! You know what those Mexican courts are like. Mightn't even have decided yet.'

McAdam smiled and nodded, thrust out his hand. 'No hard feelin's?'

'None.'

They shook briefly and, as Hunter made to move down Cedar Street, McAdam said, 'What d'you think'll happen if and when he does ask and you say no?'

'Damn! You do know what that word 'persistent' means, don't you?' The sheriff shrugged, half-smiling. 'Let's just say it's somethin' to keep that brain of yours busy trying to figure it out. Gotta use the ol' grey matter or you'll go senile, you know.'

Hunter waved briefly and strode on down Cedar, whistling softly.

'*Aggravatin*'!' McAdam muttered. '*Damn aggravatin*'!'

★ ★ ★

'And just what the devil d'you think you're doing!'

Hunter had tapped the new chisel carefully under the edge of the small wooden panel he had found in a rear corner of his room — a corner that he judged would share a common angle or support with some part of the structure above: the so-called 'tower' as he had come to think of it.

He turned sharply at Tess Deacon's demand, the head of the small hammer he had bought wrapped around with a rag so as not to make any undue noise.

But apparently there had been enough for Tess to hear and come up to investigate. She did not look pleased, but he was getting used to her disapproval of just about anything he did lately.

'Noticed this looked kind of too neat, way it was set in to this corner — not screwed in, but tight enough to need a chisel or knife blade to prise it out.'

'And why are you doing that? This is my house and you have no right to dismantle any part of it.'

'Well, mebbe you're right, but this looks to me as if it's connected in some way to that little tower thing up there.'

'And if it is, it will stay that way! I don't want anything touched. That damn — thing — up there has been bolted to part of my roof and if it's disturbed, it can easily warp some of the timbers and allow the rain or bad weather to get into this part of the house and do who knows what damage.'

Hunter looked at her. She was sure angry, but then she was always angry with him, whatever he did or said. He was getting tired of it and suddenly turned to the panel and pried with

105

the chisel, putting pressure on the handle. Wood creaked and there was a small splintering sound as the bottom of the panel protruded past its frame. She lunged forward to stop him but he exerted more pressure on the chisel and the panel, about eight by ten inches, dropped out past the rim of its framework. Hunter caught it deftly.

'No damage,' he said. 'That'll fit back in there and I can make it look more like part of the wall.'

'You damn fool!' Her breathing punctuated each word and he saw her hands clenched down at her sides. 'Oh, that awful stale air! Why're you doing this? If Will Bardon expects me to put up with some ... fool who enjoys defacing my property — '

Hunter held up the panel now, set down the hammer and squinted into the cavity. He pressed his face closer, straining to see up into the darkness of the space he had revealed. It smelled stale, all right, musty, with a hint of animal. 'Seems to be some kinda handle here.'

'Don't touch it!' Then she gave a small scream and leapt back. '*Ugh*! A spider!'

Hunter almost smiled as he used the hammer head to squash the rather small hairy thing that scuttled out of the shadows. The wood he could see formed the crossbar of a T-shaped handle and he grabbed it, tried to tug on it but it resisted solidly. Aware of the girl admonishing him not to do anything at all, he twisted the cross bar anyway, felt it move a little. He tightened his grip and put more effort into shifting it.

There was a small screech which made Tess move back quickly, and then a section of the wall in this angle of the room protruded an inch or two.

'Oh, damn you! There'll be rats and God knows what else! Why can't you leave things alone when I tell you?'

'Deaf in one ear,' he murmured, as a gust of musty gritty air hit him in the face. Other small things pattered down on his head, too, and he had no doubt she was right about rats inhabiting the space, although there was no living signs of the rodents now, just their leavings.

They were both looking upwards now, squeezing into the corner, seeing daylight above through gaps in warped timber and perhaps a loose shingle on the small pitched roof. He turned to look at her, idly brushing the dust off his clothes, wincing as the movement aggravated his wounds.

'I somehow got the impression that this Rosa was a large woman, but there's not much room up there.'

'Rosa was very small, actually, only about five feet three or four and weighed no more than ninety pounds. But she had boundless energy and a capacity for devilment. You know she used to amuse herself with that darn slingshot of hers. When she tired of shooting pigeons or other birds, she'd sometimes deliberately start popping windows in the council offices and even the county building itself. She always paid for the repairs but then she'd go and do it all over again . . . and you know how hard it is to get glass way out here.'

'Must've been a damn good shot.'

'She was. Once, when the banker — that was his office at the time, that second window with the crescent-shaped coloured glass piece . . . ? Well, for some reason she was at odds with the banker, took a light rifle — .22 calibre, I think, someone said — and shot his inkstand to pieces on his desk. Shattered the window he'd installed with imported coloured glass and ruined much of his legal work. It was her swan-song, virtually. She was heavily fined, threatened with jail and complained this lousy town just didn't have a sense of humour. Well, she found herself another man to comfort her then moved out. I don't think anyone has ever heard of her since.'

'Sounds like a crack-brain to me. See

the slats nailed across up there so she could climb into the tower itself? I dunno if I could make it now with my back, but if I did, reckon I'd have to crouch double up there, curl up like a cat. I guess it wouldn't be any chore for someone small like you described, but — '

'Look!' The girl seemed to suddenly realize she had been engaged in virtually friendly conversation with Hunter and the knowledge made her angry. 'This is my place! I admit I can use the extra money Will Bardon is paying me to house you here, but I'm not that desperate that I won't have you evicted if you do not do what I say! — I want this entrance sealed off! It stinks! You can feel the dampness. If we get our usual summer storms, now you've so conveniently broken the seal, this room and who knows how much more of my house, will be flooded!' She stepped back, hands on her hips now. 'I — I am *ordering* you to seal up that entrance at once! If you do not, I swear

I will not only have you thrown out, but *thrown in jail*!'

Hunter was mildly surprised at her rage and held up both hands, palms out.

'OK, OK! I guess I had no right, but I was just curious and didn't think there'd be any harm in looking. I'll put things back as they were. I've had a lot of different jobs over the years and I know carpentry pretty well. That's how I spotted that panel.'

'And, when you do fix things, damn well *leave* them that way!'

She almost stamped her foot, but he could see she got some pleasure in having the last word and he said nothing as she stormed out of the room.

He blew out his cheeks in a long breath as he hefted the hammer and chisel.

That was some woman! But she'd drive a man crazy . . .

★　★　★

111

Of course, he couldn't resist.

He just had to see what was up there in that cramped space now he had opened a way up. He took off his new shirt and made sure his wounds were covered with the bandages, removed his boots and contorted his body as he reached up and screwed that T-piece handle around. Up there sunlight gushed in as a small entrance door creaked open.

There was a stink he didn't like. He covered his lower face with a neckerchief and, grunting and cursing by turns, he writhed in far enough to grasp the lower slat and pulled himself up.

It cost him plenty in sweat and effort but in a few minutes he heaved himself up far enough to sit on the floor of the tower, legs dangling down towards his room below. He could kneel, but it was too cramped to stand.

There was much evidence of animal habitation though it seemed old now. He struck a match, hoping there were no snakes coiled up in a corner.

Nothing alive — except himself.

Kneeling still, he looked through some slats on two of the walls. It gave him a truncated view of the distant county buildings and that speaking platform behind which the banker had once had his office. He smiled: that damn crazy Rosa must have had herself one helluva time up here! He was almost sorry he had never met her . . . *almost.* There was a small flap that opened out, propped on a stick still attached with a dusty leather thong. His feet crunched on pebbles scattered on the floor: Rosa's ammunition supply. She could have used her slingshot to send those missiles through windows, on to the iron roofs of two small stores — what a clatter it would make in the middle of the night! — or even flick horses using the street, on the rumps, causing chaos with the riders or buckboard teams, whichever she chose.

'Plumb loco woman!' he murmured aloud with a half smile. Satisfied now, but still wondering at Rosa's warped sense of humour, he made his way down the firmly attached climbing slats.

He groaned when he saw how much debris he had loosened and the mess it had made in this rear part of his room. *Only one thing for it: he would have to clean it up and hopefully before Tess saw it!*

He almost made it: he had cornered one of the Indian maids and gave her his best green neckerchief. She would not agree to do any of the scrubbing, but brought him a bucket of hot sudsy water and a mop. He set about cleaning up his room: just like swamping out some of the saloons he had worked in.

Naturally, some of the slops filtered through the floorboards — and got Tess Deacon's attention. She came through the door with such a crash he thought she had dehinged it. But when she saw him sweating, blood trickling down his back from a few of the buckshot wounds and the area he had already cleaned, she stared.

'So you just had to go and check it for yourself.'

'I've cleaned it out. No more rat droppings — or spiders. You can even see the natural grain of the wood now . . . Cleanest it's been since it was set up. You want to take a look?' He gestured to the small climbing chute but she gave him a curled lip and an emphatic shake of her head.

'Just carry on.' After a short pause she added, 'You're doing a good job.'

He blinked as she made her way back to the open door. Then she turned and surprised him again: 'When you're ready, I'll put fresh bandages over those wounds — at least you had enough sense not to wear one of your new shirts.'

She turned and left — and he still wasn't sure whether he had heard right nor not.

Hell, for a couple of minutes, she had been almost downright civil to him.

9

Cattleman

The saloon bar fell silent as Hunter pushed through the batwings, paused briefly, and looked around.

It was his second night patrol and he saw it was going to be different from the first — yet maybe not that different. He was still under 'test', and these cowboys looked tough — and expectant.

The bar was crowded and rowdy. He had seen the several dusty horses tethered at the hitch rail outside and, as he had been passing across the open double doors of the livery down the street earlier, Lester had stepped out.

'Got me some extra customers. They went down to the saloon. Think they're eager to meet you.'

'Many?'

'Mebbe a dozen — Roy Severin's the boss man. He'll be there — and he'll have a couple of his hard boys close by. They gotta see if you're as tough as they been hearin'.'

'Thanks, Lester. Buy you a drink next time you're in the saloon.'

Lester grinned with his crooked teeth catching some of the fading light from the sundown. 'You betcha. Severin might rile you some but ain't likely he'll do any fightin' — he keeps his ramrod, Ben Slade, for that. One hard *hombre*.'

Leaving the batwings swing to behind him now, Hunter started towards the bar under the stares of the cowmen and a few locals, all hoping for some kind of action.

Roy Severin was easy to pick out: big and rugged, heavy shoulders, greying hair showing under his pushed-back hat, an arrogant stare in a bronzed outdoor face. The deputy looked casually around the room, bringing his gaze slowly back to the rancher.

The cowman nudged the blocky man

117

with the thin, unshaven face beside him. He spoke loudly. 'Be on your best behaviour, Ben, I believe a representative of the law's just arrived.'

'That what it is?' Ben Slade said arching his eyebrows. He was shorter than Severin, heavy with muscle. 'Thought it was just some saddlebum hopin' someone'll buy him a drink.' He looked hard at Hunter, challenging.

The deputy sauntered up to stand a couple of feet from Slade, who straightened quickly, eyes suddenly very wary.

'How about you? Like to buy me a drink?'

Slade was a mite taken aback, had to look up a little at Severin who smiled crookedly. Slade's axe-blade face was alert, his body tensed, at the unexpected confrontation.

'Heard lawmen weren't s'posed to drink on duty.'

'Depends what they're drinkin'.' Hunter looked past the big shoulder to the barkeep. 'Got a beer there, Stack?'

'Comin' right up, Deputy.'

Hunter managed to shoulder his way against the bar, forcing Severin and Slade apart so as to give him room. As he reached for the frothing beer glass, left-handed, he said, 'Must have half your crew with you tonight, Mr Severin.'

'Not quite half — so?'

'So just keep a tight rein on 'em — I'll give a little slack. I been a range hand and know what it's like to hit town after a few weeks looking at a cow's rear end.' He lifted the glass in a brief salute and drank. 'Like one?'

Severin was frowning, blinked at the invitation. 'I don't drink that stuff! I'm a whiskey man.'

'Well, I got enough credit to stand you one whiskey — if you want it.'

Roy Severin wiped a bent finger back and forth across the end of his big nose, a strange gesture. 'I don't like bein' beholden to lawmen.'

'Yeah, can get a bit awkward. You and your crew staying in town overnight?'

119

'Haven't quite decided yet — I likely will. Always keep a couple rooms on reserve at the hotel.'

'That meant to impress me?'

Severin stiffened and Ben Slade set down his drink and stepped away from the bar. Hunter looked at him coldly and the foreman's bronzed forehead creased a little as he glanced at his boss. 'Down, boy,' Hunter said quietly.

Slade's eye widened and his fists clenched as Roy said, 'I don't need to impress someone like you, Hunter. I'm a big man in this valley. Bigger than you'll ever be.'

Hunter nodded, set down his beer. 'You're probably right, but just now, I'm the big man in here, an' that includes your watchdog.' He jerked his head briefly at the tense Slade. 'Pat him on the head and tell him go lie down.'

'You call me a dog?' growled Slade starting to crowd Hunter, who held his ground, looking straight into the ramrod's eyes.

Severin started his crooked smile

again, but froze it at the sudden look that twisted Slade's face. The cattle boss glanced down and stiffened when he saw Hunter's cocked sixgun rammed into Slade's midriff.

'Hell almighty! Where'd that come from?' Severin couldn't stop himself voicing his surprise: he hadn't even seen the deputy's hand move.

'If the collar fits, friend . . . ' Hunter said to Slade.

Now, taken completely by surprise, Ben half-lifted his hands. 'Hey! Easy, mister!'

'Yeah, it's easy — I can do it over and over again and not even work up a sweat . . . 'Course, if I start shootin', I gotta put a mite more effort into it.'

Slade swallowed, the sound audible in the suddenly silent bar. 'No need for this, man!'

'I'll decide. But you're right, I'm showin' off. Not looking for trouble. Just want to make sure you fellers ain't thinking you'll hoo-raw the town and show the new boy what rough tough *hombres* you are — or think you are.'

'My men don't often get out of hand, Hunter,' growled Severin, annoyed that his voice sounded a little raspy.

'Make tonight one of them times and we'll all sleep easy. OK?'

'You dunno who you're takin' on here, feller,' Severin told him quietly, a growl in his words. *He had to make some sort of stand! So far all points had gone to this damn lawman.*

'Sure I do. You heard of the little excitement here in town and figured you'd better come on in and get things sorted out the way you want 'em. Well, I got no beef about a range crew letting down their hair — within reason. But *I'm* the one decides. See, the town's mine while I'm on patrol, and I'm here to see the ordinances and the laws are followed. Might bend 'em a little here and there — how far is kinda up to you and your crew. Now I reckon Stack there might even run to buyin' you boys one round of drinks. In return, you behave yourselves; don't rough up the gals; take your fights out into the alley. I'll look in again shortly, see how the night's progressing.' He looked at Roy Severin, whose face was only six inches from him. 'What you say, range boss?'

Severin ran his tongue around his lips. His voice was strained, but he met and held the deputy's gaze. 'You're either bendin' over backwards to be fair, or tryin' to hide that we got you buffaloed.'

Hunter grinned without much warmth. 'I've done a heap of buffalo huntin'.'

'Well, you seem like you wanna play fair, so we'll meet you halfway, but there could be other times when we won't be so accommodatin'.'

Hunter's cold smile widened a little.

'Sure, I savvy that.' He holstered the weapon with a smooth movement. 'Put it away for now, keep it for one of them not-so-accommodatin' nights mebbe. Have your fun, boys, but be outta town by sun-up.' That brought a howl of protests. Ignoring them,

Hunter nodded to Severin and left casually.

'Jesus!' Ben Slade said hoarsely. 'That scary bastard's got my shirt collar all wet with sweat!'

Roy Severin's collar was too, but he wasn't about to admit it. Fuming, he went to see Will Bardon soon after Hunter left the saloon and its mighty tense atmosphere.

'Judas Priest, Will! What kinda *hombre* you hire for chief deputy here! Christ, he's in town for three days and we got three men to bury! Couple days later when I bring my crew in, he has half of 'em wettin' their pants — and all he did was poke his gun into Ben Slade's belly!'

Will Bardon looked up from the paper he was studying and set it down on his desk. He could hear the genuine concern in the big cattleman's voice.

'Take it easy, Roy. He's the best man for the job. Oh, yeah, he's a killer, but as long as he's on our side when he does his killing, I've got no complaint.'

'Well, I tell you, he had me sweatin'!'

Bardon smiled. 'He's that kind of man — but we still need him.'

'You sure?'

Bardon, sober now, tapped the paper he had been studying. 'Damn sure! Stage just brought me this from that lousy, do-gooder 'watchdog', as he calls himself, in Santa Fe — our old friend Ashley Lyon. Says here he doesn't see any point in Cimarron Valley being declared a separate county, let alone possibly expanding into an independent *state*. Not in his lifetime — and he's coming up to tell us so to our faces. Make it official. And that'll mean no head taxes.'

Severin eased down into a chair across the desk from Bardon. 'Thought you had all that tied up? Hell, I've been workin' my butt off, rode . . . must've been two hundred miles, all over the country, and back into the ranges, signin' up the ranches to ship their beef through our pass. They'll do it, long as we keep our head tax at a reasonable level. None of 'em want to pay any kinda tax, but I made it sound like each one had a special deal and he should keep it to himself, or everyone would want the same.' He half-smiled and winked. 'Little bit of larceny appeals to most folks.'

'It's the goddamn head tax that's made Lyon balk! Says it'll stir up 'old and bitter memories'. He's talking about the time when the Yankees moved in right after the war and ruined almost every rancher in the South with their damn taxes: first it was a man's steers, then his land, then his crops — more cows and acres he owned, more it cost him. Wiped out most. Lyon's family was one, but somehow he managed to get into politics and now he's plenty powerful.'

'But that tax was years ago!'

Bardon's eyes were cold. 'Men down here got long memories, you oughta know that, Roy, the way your kin suffered.'

Severin nodded, face grim. 'Yeah!

126

Lot of folk moved here in the first place hoping to dodge the damn taxes. Instead, they got smacked in the teeth with a bunch of others that were worse.'

'Now, if Lyons reminds 'em — ' Bardon shook his head sharply. 'Won't do us a whole lot of good then whether our tax is high or low, he'll just declare it illegal.'

'Hell, you explain to Lyons he'll get his share?'

Bardon shook his head slowly. 'He's a buttoned-up-tight Christian now.' Bardon spat accurately into a spittoon on his side of the desk. 'He's literally 'got religion', and he says he's been nominated for land administrator.' He slammed a fist down on to the desk, the thud making pens and papers jump. 'That means he's got a lot of powerful people behind him and he's wantin' to show 'em they did the right thing by making him a commissioner. We'll never get him to agree to us charging for the trail drivers usin' our pass. All that goddamn work for nothing!' He paused to catch his breath which was coming in sharp gusts now. 'If ever we do become a county sometime, as we grow, we won't have any say in taxes — We'll be *payin'* 'em along with everyone else!'

Severin frowned. 'Well, how in the hell did it get to that point, Will? And, what's more important, what're we gonna do about it?'

Bardon gave him a small smile. 'I have a glimmer of an idea. You came in here thundering about Deputy Hunter — '

'Oh, yeah! And I want somethin' done about him and pronto. I've invested too damn much in this already without havin' to pull my horns in now just because some ranny who's slick with a gun is gonna tell me what I can and can't do.'

'Roy, the way I've got things figured, Hunter might well be the key to this whole deal.'

Severin shook his head savagely. 'I dunno what the hell you're talkin' about! But you brought him here and it's up to you to — '

'I *know* what it's up to me to do, Roy! You're on the outside and *don't* know what's going to happen and it riles you. OK. But mebbe it's best that way for now.'

'You'll have to gimme more'n that, Will.'

Bardon stared hard across his desk, saw there was no retreat in the rancher. *He'd either have to tell him or lose him*, and *that* was not an option.

He needed Severin to get the original plan underway.

The big rancher's apparent ready agreement to pay a nominal head tax on his own vast herds that would use the new pass was essential to influence the other ranchers. Roy was regarded by them as being wise and prosperous, so his decisions were worth close consideration. It was almost a foregone conclusion that the other valley ranchers would follow Severin's lead — whichever way he jumped.

It worked out pretty much as

planned, with almost every rancher within a hundred miles signing up. Ten cents a head on their cattle sounded mighty reasonable — and was — but multiplied by tens of thousands of cows lumbering through that pass, *hundreds* of thousands in the course of a season — well, someone's bank account was going to grow, and quickly.

But if Roy Severin gave the proposal his seal of approval that would be good enough for the others. Still, Lyon, a charismatic man noted for his integrity, could declare the head tax illegal because the pass was on state land . . . *and,* Lyon casually mentioned that not only could he divert any tax to the state, but the men who made the pass could be open to all kinds of legal penalties for acting on their own initiative.

There were egos here, or in the state administration, that Will Bardon had simply ignored. Now he was going to feel the pressure as they asserted themselves and reminded him that

Cimarron Valley was still under their jurisdiction.

So Bardon *needed* Severin, more than ever now with the threat of Lyon's hovering.

He stood abruptly and went to a cupboard and brought out a glittering cut-glass decanter of brandy with a little oval silver label around the neck on a short chain.

'My best brandy, for the best deal you'll ever hear, Roy! Let's drink to that and I'll spell it out for you.'

10

Celebration

'What've you been doin'?'

Hunter looked up from the glass of beer he was toying with, sitting alone at a table near a corner of the saloon.

The sheriff was standing there, hands loosely at his sides, face unsmiling. Hunter frowned briefly — on-off — *He had not detected any levity in the lawman's question.*

'Me? You can see. Had breakfast after the night shift, went for a walk around the town and decided to have a drink before turning in for a sleep.' He toed a chair out towards McAdam. 'Siddown, Mac, you look bothered.'

McAdam kept his sober look as he eased down into the chair, took out his new pipe and groped for a vesta. Hunter slid one across the table, waited patiently while the lawman lit up and a cloud of blue tobacco smoke suspended itself over the table.

'You might've stood on someone's toes without knowing it,' McAdam suggested quietly.

Hunter smiled. 'I'd know it . . . so would they.'

'I b'lieve it.'

'Well? What's the beef? And who by?'

'Dunno. No, really don't. Only that Will Bardon himself called me to his office and said to tell you he wanted to see you there 'without delay'!'

'What the hell? He knows I'm just comin' off shift.'

'I ask again: what've you been up to?'

Hunter shrugged, drained his beer. 'Better go and find out. I can't think of anything — except I kinda nudged Severin and his crew a little.'

'Hell, that was expected. If you hadn't I'd say that was why Will wants to see you.'

'I'll let you know.'

Hunter stood, adjusted his sixgun rig

a little more comfortably on his hip and, with a terse nod to the sheriff, headed for the batwings.

He soon found out why Will Bardon had sent for him.

The first thing the man did was glance up from some papers he was reading, looking a mite annoyed at the interruption. Then suddenly the expression left his face and he smiled pleasantly, gesturing to the visitor's chair.

'Ah, good of you to come so soon, Hunter, if I'd realized you'd just come off night shift, I'd have left it a little later.'

The hell you would've, Hunter thought. He was beginning to know the council chairman's devious ways.

He dropped into the chair and thumbed back his hat, accepted a cheroot from a decorated plywood box and lit up.

Bardon leaned back at his ease, elbows on his chair arms, fingertips to fingertips. 'Just how good are you with that gun?'

Hunter kept his face blank and shrugged. 'Not as good as those tricks in the tent-show made me look.'

Bardon leaned forward slightly, definite interest in his eyes now. 'You're saying the show was basically a set of tricks?'

'Well, yeah. Shooting shot glasses out of the air and so on, was all arranged with enough cover for the stooge to toss the glasses up, but at an angle so that the audience couldn't see the catgut line attached. It was very fine and all happened too fast anyway. Mostly a matter of timing on my part — I had to practise like hell, use blanks in my gun, always fired very quickly, twice, in case my timing was a little off. It had to happen as soon as the glass reached the top of its rise. If I fired too early, before the line stretched taut and exploded the glass with a detonator cap set in the bottom, my second shot covered up. The audience were only looking at the exploding glass by then.'

Bardon's eyes were narrowed now,

his hands on the arms of his chairs, fingers gripping firmly. 'You must've had a very good sense of timing.'

'Lotsa practice. Might've messed up once in a while but the presenter, as he liked to call himself, always managed to cover with some weak joke.'

'But you did other acts with your gun, didn't you? Shooting twigs set at various distances in the ground, eggs on top of hollowed sticks, necks of empty bottles, even small balls rolling down a slope.'

Someone's done their homework! Hunter thought.

Hunter's look was narrowed now. 'You been readin' one of the programmes?'

'Yes — Roy Severin's bronc-buster had one. He'd seen your tent show in Bisbee one time.'

'All right, but I'm a much better shot with a rifle than I am with a sixgun; except at close range, a lot of those shots you mentioned were made with a Winchester.'

Bardon leaned forward eagerly, eyes brightening. 'No tricks? Just you and your rifle?'

Hunter nodded. 'You can't trick the audience all the time. There were a lot of sober folk out there as well as half-drunk cowboys and drifters. And using a rifle meant the targets had to be on open ground — no hiding a stooge.'

'You're not just deliberately putting yourself down?'

Hunter shook his head, just once, but emphatically. 'Nor am I patting myself on the back, just trying to tell it like it is — was. Where're we going with this, Councillor?'

Bardon took time out to take a cigar from an ornate silver box, cut it, pierce it, light it. 'It so happens that we — the town — are going to be honoured with a visit from the man who's going to be the new state land administrator — one Commissioner Ashley Lyon. You've no doubt heard of him?'

'If I have, I've forgotten.'

'Well, he's the man who oversees the state land and makes sure it's put to the best possible use — that means for the good of the state, which comes first, private enterpsise somewhere down the list: a *long way* down.' He didn't bother to try to hide his bitterness. 'You get the idea. Well, he's coming to Cimarron Valley, and soon.'

He took a deep drag on his cigar and expelled most of the smoke before adding, in a quieter voice, 'The thing is, Hunter, a few of us businessmen took advantage of a landslide in the Cataracts last winter. We pitched in and blasted and dragged away all the rubble, and found that with a little more blasting, and a change of direction, we could make a pass clear through the range. So we did it.'

'The pass the local ranchers are gonna use to get their herds to market this season — yeah, Mac told me.'

Bardon didn't like being interrupted but nodded curtly. 'Well, we — rightfully so, I believe — decided we were entitled to some compensation for all our work.'

'Seems fair.'

'So we decided to charge a small tax on any cattle using the pass. And any rancher with brains *would* use it, saving extra miles of driving through hard country and gettin' his cows to market in better condition. Everyone gaining all round.'

'And you collecting it, of course.'

Bardon nodded, smile fading slowly: just a little wary now as he realized how quickly this gunfighter was catching on, even getting ahead of him. He sighed.

'Naturally. But our commissioner from the state capitol sees it differently. New broom and all that. He sees it only that we opened that pass without official permission from the Lands Department, and didn't even use a state engineer. Maybe they had other plans for it, I don't know, but he's coming here to chastise us, I believe, perhaps even confiscate the pass we made and put it under his control.'

'And you and your friends won't be able to make your fortunes.'

Will Bardon's face was stern now. 'Yes; we feel it's our right to claim recompense, but if the state decides to take over . . . ' He let it hang, spreading his hands.

'Reckon that'd rile the hell outa me.'

The chairman's smile was suddenly back. 'Quite!'

'But how do I fit in?'

'Straight from the shoulder, eh?' Bardon paused and gave a small laugh just to let Hunter know he was only kidding when he added, 'I'd *like* to say 'Go and shoot the son of a bitch!', but that'd be just a shade too drastic, eh?'

'Reckon so.' There was nothing to tell from Hunter's toneless comment just what he really thought.

'Of course. But we thought there'd be no harm in — well — pandering to the administrator a little, bend over backwards to give him a visit that's quite pleasant, even memorable. In other words, make him glad he came, and make sure his feeling toward us is a warm one . . . Oh, no, no, no! I can see you're thinking in terms of — er — 'accommodating' ladies, lots of free booze and so on, but our man is a devout Christian. Stuck away in the Capitol, he's probably not aware of how tough life can be out here so we want to show him, with a big Cimarron welcome. A little rough riding, perhaps, a small cattle round-up and branding, a chuck-wagon race through the streets — then pack the town square outside there with enthusiastic crowds, for him to make his speech — and hope that we've put him in a good mood so he won't treat us too harshly.'

'Like stopping your tax?'

Bardon held up a hand. 'Naturally, that's the prime reason for the welcome. Now, what I'd like you to do, as your contribution, is to give us a demonstration of your prowess with your guns: after all, you are our chief deputy.'

Hunter sat up straighter. 'I already

told you those things were carefully arranged.'

'Yes, yes, I understand. Forget shooting glasses out of the air, there're still pot-shotting playing cards, empty bottles and other things you mentioned. You said you're better with a rifle than a handgun, well, that's fine, use your rifle — or anything else! As long as you pull off something good enough to please the commissioner ... I think he's somewhat anti-firearm but some spectacular target shooting should entertain him adequately. What d'you say?'

Hunter looked uncertain and the chairman added, 'Of course, you'll be paid, and quite well: more than for being our chief deputy.' He smiled tightly. 'That's show-business style, isn't it? High rewards for a good performance.' He leaned forward suddenly. 'That head tax is our right, Hunter!'

'I savvy, Councillor, but it takes time to get things set up for something like you're asking me to do.'

'Of course, you'll have leave from

your deputy duties to do that — and time off to practise if you need it. Yours will be a pivotal role in this, I assure you.'

*　*　*

He was back in the saloon at the corner table again, drinking a whiskey and chasing it down with beer, when McAdam came in. Hunter yawned, feeling tired now after the night shift.

'Was it that boring a session with Will?' the sheriff asked, dropping into a chair and signalling the barkeep to bring two more whiskies with beer chasers.

'Just feelin' weary. I can see you're bustin' to find out what Bardon wanted.' McAdam tried to shrug it off as something that didn't bother him one way or another, but he listened intently when Hunter began to speak.

The sheriff looked steadily at Hunter when he had finished. 'What'd you say?'

'What d'you think? I can use the

money and it's no chore to do a little fancy pot-shotting. You know this Lyon feller?'

'He was up here once sorting out some land dispute, even before he became an official commissioner. Not everybody was happy with his decision, but he was stubborn: they had to do what he said — and he had the authority to back it up. Heard he's toughened up even more since he got into politics full-time.'

'Well, if they wanta try to keep him happy, I guess I can do my part.'

'Did he say when Lyon's due?'

'No, but I've got time off to practise. I'd guess it won't be too long before he arrives. Bardon's pretty damn edgy.'

'Stands to lose a heap, I guess. Oh, and your friend and mine, Ollie Reeves, is back in town, by the by.'

'He'd best stay clear of me.'

McAdam shrugged. 'He's been out at Roy Severin's spread. Dunno why . . . them two never did get along too well. Queer, ain't it?'

Hunter shrugged.

'They tell me there was quite a bit of shootin' going on, too, like someone practising. Rifle and pistol. What d'you make of that?'

Hunter reached slowly for his brimming whiskey glass. 'I dunno, but mebbe I better give it some thought.'

11

High Noon Marksman

Hunter was concentrating on converting a bullet into a dum-dum on the small balcony outside his room when he heard his name called.

Squinting through the narrow rails he was surprised to see Tess Deacon standing in the yard, looking up at him.

'What on earth are you doing?'

'Working.'

'But that endless dull sort of screeching sound — are you cutting metal or something?'

'Close. I'm a converting a copper-cased bullet into a dum-dum.'

He saw her stiffen, her face straighten. 'Dum-dum? Isn't that some form of terrible bullet that causes such terrible injuries?'

He almost smiled at the note of

disapproval. 'That's what they say.'

'Look, Hunter, I don't approve of you in many ways but isn't this a little much — even for you?'

'Been using 'em for years, in the tent show, but not in the war. It was the nearest brick wall and a firing squad if the army caught you with one. There're some rules, even when your job is to kill the enemy.'

'And you're breaking them!'

He had to grin and saw it made her even angrier. He stood and leaned through the rails showing her the cartridge and half-finished bullet. He reached, fumbled another from his belt loop. 'This is how they normally look — I'm just cutting away some of the copper sheathing to expose the lead. I'll flatten the tip, maybe round the edges a trifle, so it'll make a larger hole.'

'And what will that do? Blow a man's arm off?'

He tried to keep a straight face at her rising anger. He swiftly held up a hand as she took a deep breath, ready to upbraid him. 'I'm not going to use it on anyone.'

'Oh, God, you're not going to mangle some poor defenceless animal!'

'You sure do have a low opinion of me, Tess! I want a dum-dum for knocking knots out of a circle of sawn log that I'll be using as a target.'

She froze with her mouth half-open, frowning.

'Bardon wants me to put on a shooting act as part of the entertainment for Lyon. I've done it before and I usually shoot at chunks with knots sawn from a log. I punch 'em out with flat-nosed bullets, make a face for the kids — ordinary-shaped slugs only splinter or dig in without anything spectacular happening. Dum-dums take 'em right out.'

Her teeth tugged at her bottom lip. 'If I thought you had deliberately led me into making a fool of myself . . . '

He quickly covered by picking up another cartridge with a bullet that had been filed almost to a needle point.

'This is the other side of the coin. Filed to a very fine point for coring apples.'

For a moment she stood, half-frowning. 'You're making fun of me! Core an apple with a bullet?'

'I have my off days, but mostly I manage it.'

Her scepticism was barely hidden as she said, 'You must have remarkable eyesight! Unless you hold the gun muzzle against the apple!'

'Usually shoot from about five or six yards — depends on the size of the apple.'

'I still think you're amusing yourself at my expense, Hunter! Well, I am *not* amused!'

As she stormed away, hair swirling, he called, 'Come see the show. Mebbe you'll get a laugh out of it if I miss.'

She didn't pause or acknowldge the invitation. He chuckled, went back to shaping his dum-dum.

★ ★ ★

He was cleaning and oiling his rifle's action when she appeared again, some half-hour later, on the town-side of the rooming-house, staring up at him through the rails.

As he worked the lever he saw her. She looked uncomfortable but somehow determined.

'I-I believe I owe you some thanks.'

He struck his forehead with the heel of his hand. 'Now, what could I have done to warrant such a momentous decision?'

She drew down and released a deep breath. 'All right! I suppose I deserved that!'

He laughed as she started to turn away, miffed. 'Thanks for the 'thanks' whatever they were for.'

She froze, turned back, lips compressed, face reddening, getting herself under control. But her voice was quite calm when she spoke again:

'Will Bardon sent for me. He offered me the catering concession for Ashley Lyon's welcoming picnic.'

'Let's hope he's hungry.'

She seemed flustered. 'I-I have to thank you for suggesting to Bardon that he give me the concession. I can certainly use the money. It's been a hard year. So, thank you.'

She started away and he said, absently working the lever action he had just oiled, 'I'm glad for you, Tess.'

She nodded tersely and he saw her gaze was on the rifle. 'That looks just a little different to most rifles. Sounds different, too, when you work the lever that way. Much quieter than others I've heard.'

'No slack in the action,' he explained. 'The tolerances are at least twice as fine as those in an off-the-rack Winchester.'

'You had it made specially?'

'No-ooo. It wasn't made for me — I came by it a couple of years ago. The man who owned it had it built for his son's twenty-first birthday, but a rustler shot the kid in the back. I saw it, and squared things when I finally caught up with the rustler. The old man gave me the special rifle. And if I'm a good shot, a lot of it's because of the fine work that's gone into its making.'

'Heavens! Modesty!' She sighed. 'You are a surprising man, Hunter . . . ' Her words drifted off and she added, 'It's too bad you're a killer, too.'

'I can live with that.'

'Yes, I expect you can. It'll be interesting to see what Commissioner Lyon thinks of our town — having a killer for a deputy sheriff. I'm not sure his Christian beliefs will approve.'

'I don't always sleep very well, Tess, but I'm damn sure that thought won't keep me awake.'

*   *   *

The entire crowd of gawkers who had followed Hunter out on to the flats beyond the town clapped wildly, and a few yelled, as the needle-nosed bullet sliced through the big red apple without blowing it apart, just leaving a neatly drilled tunnel through the fruit.

The apple hit the grassy slope beneath the wooden framework Hunter had built to hold a set of six apples — with a variety of sizes. Only the two smallest had exploded when the specially shaped bullets hit slightly off-line.

The four larger ones were perfectly cored, held up by excited kids who were asked to do so by Roy Severin, who was practising his upcoming role as master of ceremonies.

'Anyone want to invite Deputy Hunter for breakfast?' the rancher called. 'You should see him peel an orange! Takes him about half a magazine! 'Course, it's best if you eat out of doors when you invite him to your table!'

He got a surpringly big laugh from the audience.

This wasn't the official performance — Ashley Lyon and his entourage had not yet arrived in Cimarron. This was a rehearsal, not just for Hunter and his rifle — though that was the most popular — but also for other entertainers who had various acts to perform and perfect.

The crowds were happy at the free show, many surprised at the hitherto hidden humour of Roy Severin, the usually stern-faced, no-nonsense rancher.

Sheriff McAdam handed the sweating Hunter a large glass mug of frothing beer and the deputy downed it in a few grateful gulps. There was quite a crowd gathering around the lawmen now, most interested in Hunter. Everyone wanted to examine his Winchester, but while he would demonstrate its smoothness and accuracy, explain its flip-up vernier scale rear sight, he did not relinquish his hold on the weapon.

'What'sa matter, Hunter?' slurred Ollie Reeves, the reek of whiskey mixing with the sweat of his grubby shirt. 'Figure someone'll see it's a trick rifle?'

'And what sort of tricks would it do, Ollie?' Hunter asked, getting some pleasure at seeing the blotchy face of the other man, fading reminders of that gun-whipping.

'Well, I dunno! But there has to be some trick to shootin' the core outa an apple!' He looked around blearily. 'Huh? Whoever heard of such a thing?'

'*Heard* about it! We *seen* it, Ollie!' someone answered with a laugh. 'Where the hell were you?'

'Drinkin' the bar dry!' someone else called, getting a good laugh.

Revell must've realized he was making a fool of himself and swore half under his breath as he roughly shoved his way through the crowd.

'I hope you can repeat it, Hunter,' Will Bardon said quietly, standing close to the deputy. 'I must say I am very impressed.'

'Lyon's the one you want impressed — when's he due to arrive?' Hunter asked.

Bardon grimaced slightly. 'Tonight — on the sundown stage. So you'll only have today to practise — if you need extra time, well, we'll just have to make it. The show is due to start at noon tomorrow, after Lyon examines the pass! So everyone'll be busy . . . and by the way, the correct title is *Commissioner* Lyon.'

He suddenly turned to the slowly dispersing crowd. 'Ladies and gents, tomorrow is the big day! The entire show will be bigger and better. Now, I want the whole town to turn up, fill the grounds, dress in your best and most colourful clothes, wave streamers and so on. Give Commissioner Lyon lots of cheers. Make it a grand arrival — he can do plenty for our town, so let him know in no uncertain way that he's welcome and popular. I want all the performers to do better than their best! Though I confess I'm not sure how Deputy Hunter here can improve on what he's showed us today. Have you ever seen anyone shoot a rifle more accurately? Eh? Well come on! How about a cheer for our top marksman? I personally doubt that you'll find another who can handle a rifle as well as our Hunter! Now, where's that cheer . . . ?'

It resounded across the flats and drifted through the fringing trees and down to the streets of Cimarron. Hunter acknowledged with a brief wave. He was pleased — it wasn't often he felt genuinely flattered, and hardly ever for his prowess with his guns.

But he wondered why Bardon kept stressing how well he shot a *rifle*, as if people couldn't see for themselves.

★ ★ ★

And they did, for the second time, when the *High Noon Howdy*, as some likkered-up range-rider christened the occasion, started on time with the entire population of the town crowding into the neatly dragged and hurriedly smoothed-down flats to overflowing.

Folk came drifting in from out beyond the Cataracts, too, some having ridden for two days with families, making trail-side camps to get there by the deadline.

Will Bardon, standing on the dais, sweating in his frock-coat and bowler-hat outfit, nudged Roy Severin who was also dressed up to the nines in striped trousers, pleated grey shirt and fancy vest, stretched up a mite to get closer to Roy's ear, and said, not without some undisguised bitterness, 'Why the hell didn't we think about charging entry? Just a quarter, even a dime! For God's sake *look* at the crowd! We could be making another fortune!'

'Our turn'll come, Will. As long as we can get that head tax approved.'

Bardon flicked his gaze down to where Commissioner Lyon stood talking to some of his staff and rubber-necking Cimarron businessmen who wanted to get their share of anything Lyon was going to offer. His rotund figure strained at the cloth of some imported outfit made of a new material that actually *sheened* like metal in the sunlight. His bald head sheened, too, with a film of sweat, which he mopped briefly with a bright blue kerchief.

'Look at that smug son of a bitch! By God, Roy, he hinted the work on the pass would need professional attention and that would put it *under Santa Fe's jurisdiction*. It's not working out *quite* the way we figured but I swear if that fat slug even hesitates to approve our tax, I'll throttle him with my own hands!'

'Now that would really be getting your hands dirty, Will!' chuckled the rancher.

Bardon, slow of wit and without much sense of humour, stared, puzzled, then his face brightened and he lightly punched big Roy on the shoulder. 'You're right there, pardner! Now, Mr Master of Ceremonies, how about getting this show under way. Grab that speaking-trumpet and *let 'er rip*!'

12

Trap

It had fallen to Hunter again to do the night patrol but Sheriff McAdam came strolling up as he left a small porch behind the hardware store, after checking the locks on the door.

Hunter heard a footstep crunch and literally took McAdam's breath away with the speed of his turning, going down on one knee and bringing up a fully cocked Colt in his right hand.

'*Whoa!* Judas Priest, man! Don't shoot! It's me!'

'Better try gnashing your teeth or break into song if you're aiming to sneak up on a man like that!' Hunter put away the gun. 'By God, I tell you, Mac, that was close!'

Mac was shaken and tried to cover by bringing out the makings and starting to build a cigarette.

'You're a bit edgy tonight, aren't you?'

'Lots of shadows moving about. Here, have a cheroot. Let's live a little.'

The sheriff led the way behind a stack of barrels. They lit up and cupped the glowing tips of their cheroots in their left hands as they smoked.

'Thought you might like a little company — or to turn in early. I can finish your shift for you, give you a chance to rest up before the show tomorrow.'

'Your wife ain't gonna invite me to supper again, I keep takin' you away.'

'She savvies. Not all that happy, mind, but she's used to my comings and goings — mostly goings.'

'You got a good woman there. Did you go meet this Lyon with Bardon and his sidekicks when the stage came?'

'I was there, sort of in the background. Lyon's put on some weight since I last saw him. Stand him beside a hogshead in the shadows and you'd be hard put to spot the right one.'

'Must be that good livin' in Santa Fe.'

Mac was silent a few seconds, looked thoughtful as the glow of his cheroot washed across his craggy features when he drew in smoke. 'I was on the fringes, like I said. He seems more arrogant since last time — or mebbe just more confident. 'Course that could be because he's in a powerful position now. He was just another politician before, but he kept Bardon in his place — whatever that is, in Lyon's view.'

'Maybe he's not as kindly disposed towards Bardon's plans for Cimarron as good ol' Will figures.'

Mac looked at him sharply. 'Bardon and Roy Severin'll throw fits seven ways to Sunday if that head tax is killed.'

'Always struck me as strange that Roy was agreeable to paying *any* tax even at a reduced rate like Bardon claimed.'

'It's all a sham! Roy's not payin' any tax: never intended to. He's just sayin' he will. It's s'posed to show folks what a fine responsible citizen he is by claiming to go along with the need for the tax, showin' 'em he's willing to do his part and pay his way along with all the other ranchers . . . *in theory!* It's meant to impress Lyon, too, of course, let him see what civic-minded folk we breed down here and hope that'll help him decide to let us run our own affairs.'

'I'll bet Bardon's workin' hard on that one.'

'Likely. I think Will has notions of headin' for a seat on the Santa Fe Executive Council some day himself.'

Hunter took a deep drag on his cheroot and dribbled the smoke out as he spoke. 'He better hope this wingding he's got planned for tomorrow impresses Lyon then.'

Mac glanced at him sharply. 'Ye-aaah. If Lyon ain't happy, well, I reckon we're gonna see more fireworks than'll be lightin' up the sky tomorrow night.'

They left it at that. Hunter refused to

let the sheriff work the rest of his shift. 'No need for it, Mac.'

'Just thought it might help — give you a good night's rest so your hands're steady.'

'I can do most of that stuff in my sleep anyway. Thanks, but no, go spend an evenin' with your wife, Mac, and you make her some supper for a change.'

Mac looked shocked. 'Me? I can't even boil water!'

Hunter laughed and strolled away with a casual wave.

Severin's crew had stayed on in town and were becoming rowdier, perhaps more than was called for or could be blamed on the booze they had consumed.

Hunter's shift was to end at midnight, his relief Ollie Revell. He was just over half an hour short of this deadline, and ready to check the saloon one more time, when there was a crash of breaking glass from behind the building, followed by loud, angry shouting.

Hunter approached quickly but cautiously, Colt in hand. He rounded a rear corner, prepared for trouble, moving so as to put a wall at his back. As he slid along, left hand feeling for the end of the building, he found there was someone already there.

He stopped dead, sucking down a sharp breath, thrusting away from the wall, and bringing his gun hand around and down. There was enough reflection from the street at the head of the alley for him to see a movement as a man closed with him. Another leapt out of the dark, pinning his gun arm against the clapboards.

'Got the sonuver!' the man grunted.

Hunter lashed out with his boots, raking the worn high heel down the leg of the one holding him. There was a scream of pain followed by an obscene curse and the grip loosened. But others were there now, and crowded the deputy back, knees lifting into his lower body. A club of some kind caught him a blow across the side of his head that

165

made his ears ring.

He dropped to one knee swiftly, putting down his left hand to steady himself briefly before thrusting up with a mighty grunt. He felt the top of his head squash someone's nose, warm blood spurting.

He was still off-balance though and they slammed him back against the wall, two men holding his arms straight out from his body, while two others jostled for position in front of him, fists hammering.

Hunter felt his legs ready to fold, braced himself as well as he could just in time to take a fist alongside the jaw and another on the opposite side of his neck. The night was beginning to spin around him, punctuated by flashes of pain as the assailants enjoyed themselves.

Even through the pain, he thought he recognized one voice.

Then there was another: one that he knew for sure.

'What the hell's going on here!'

It was McAdam, roaring, and wading in, swinging his gun barrel at heads that desperate hands tried to protect. Left — right — right again — the gun's barrel rising and falling, men grunting aloud, stumbling away, cursing.

Suddenly, Hunter was down on his knees, shoulders leaning back against the wall, swaying and bloody, as his tormentors scattered. McAdam went after them in a token pursuit but was soon back. He stepped in quickly, supporting Hunter who was leaning heavily on the clapboards, only half erect. He thrust a neckerchief into Hunter's hands and the injured man, breathing hard, mopped at his face.

'Th-thought I told you to go make your wife's supper,' Hunter slurred, and spat some blood.

'So happened she had a couple of lady friends over for a hand of bridge. Decided to come back and give you some company. Recognize any of those sons of bitches?'

Hunter looked up and the sheriff saw

one eye was closing fast, and a gash on his left cheek was oozing blood steadily. 'There was one voice I knew,' he slurred. 'Pretty sure, leastways — Ben Slade.'

'Yeah, Ben's a mean one all right. Word is you insulted him in front of Roy. Figures you felt he wasn't worth botherin' with when you called him Roy's watchdog.'

'He insults easily.'

'We-ell, that's Ben. And he's mighty mean with it.'

'I like a man with lots of confidence in himself — when he's got three, four others to back him up . . . Mac, I could sure use a drink.'

'Then let's get you inside and you can wrap your chompin' gear around a double whiskey.'

He took Hunter's arm and helped him stagger to the saloon's side door. As soon as they entered, it was obvious everyone there already knew what had happened in the alley — some may have even witnessed the beating. Or helped . . .

But Hunter only had eyes for one man standing at the end of the bar with a large whiskey in his hand, rubbing one leg absently with the other — his trouser leg was torn, bloody: Ben Slade.

The big hand holding the drink had skinned knuckles and there was a darkening patch under Ben's left eye, blood oozing from one nostril. His eyes widened and he tossed the drink down swiftly then hurled the glass at Hunter who had stepped away from the sheriff.

'Hunter! No!' McAdam snapped as his deputy went into that instinctive deadly crouch, eyes drilling into Slade, right hand hanging easily, yet somehow threateningly, close to his gun butt.

'You're plenty tough in a wolf-pack, Ben, how about now?'

'Hunter, I said — ' McAdam cut the rest of what he was going to say because it was obviously too late.

The guns came up, blazed, almost simultaneously, Hunter's a split second ahead. His shot slammed Ben six feet along the bar which had emptied swiftly once it had become clear that gunplay was inevitable. The Lazy S ramrod clawed at the bar edge, his gun jumping from his hand as it fired, the bullet gouging a splintery trough in the floor.

A moment later, Ben Slade buried his face into some of the wet sawdust which covered the floor in front of the bar, his blood staining it red.

'Hell! That makes *four* he's killed!' someone breathed and that started a murmuring among the drinkers.

'Jesus, man! Now you've done it.'

Hunter looked soberly at the sheriff. 'Fair and square, wasn't it?'

'That's as mebbe, but Bardon won't stand for this, specially with Lyon on hand! Reckon you've done yourself out of a job!'

While waiting for the doctor/undertaker, Hunter downed another whiskey, served by a shaky-looking barkeep, and suddenly felt a warm, slim hand grasp his, tugging insistently. He looked down and smiled when he saw Silver beside him.

'Come with me. Come on!'

'Hey! Wait up, Silver . . . '

The crowds were milling about and there was much talk and plenty of drinks flowing. Hunter followed the saloon girl to her small closet-like room in the shadows at the far end of the bar. She pulled him inside.

'Listen, I'm kinda busy right now, Silver . . . ' he began, noting the rumpled bed which took up most of the room. A free-standing set of three drawers jutted from a corner, a lantern turned low on the top. 'I can't take time for — '

She opened a drawer, took out some cottonwool and a metal dish which she splashed water into from a jug. 'I'll get you cleaned up some.' She reached for a bottle of cloudy fluid.

'Thanks, but it's not necessary — '

'This lotion will stop the bruising showing so much. Now just let me do this for you — please, Hunter.'

He stopped resisting her and let her go to work.

'They're after you, you know!' she whispered hoarsely. 'They've been settin' things up for ages, waitin' for you to show up on your patrol. They faked that brawl outside to bring you running — Oops! Sorry!'

Her hands were not the most gentle and he winced as she dabbed at the cuts and grazes on his face. The lotion felt soothing, but he held her hand as she made to wipe at the cut on his cheek, looking into her flushed face.

'What d'you mean they're after me?'

'All I know is I heard Roy Severin talkin' with Ben Slade earlier and he told Ben to get you into a dark corner out there and to — 'Push the bastard hard!' Those were his exact words. He added, 'And make damn sure he learns his lesson.' She chuckled softly. 'Wonder who taught who?'

He heard the smile in her voice, unable to see her clearly in the dimness of the low-set lamp. 'Thanks. Silver, that dollar of mine was well spent.'

'Aw, you still got change comin' if

ever you want to collect, Deputy . . . Any time.'

She moved closer and her plump, moist lips fastened on his mouth. He left them there for a few seconds, then twisted away, but not in any insulting way. He patted one of her buttocks.

'Thanks again, Silver, I won't forget this.'

He found McAdam waiting at the edge of the crowd as Ben Slade's body was carried out. There was no sign of Roy Severin, but other Lazy S men would have gotten word to him by now, wherever he was. Probably Bardon, too, and maybe even Lyon.

The sheriff looked grim. 'Bardon wants to see you right away.' He ran a sober gaze over Hunter. 'He sent one of his clerks down, so he obviously knows what's happened.'

'And likely that it was *gonna* happen?' asked Hunter.

'Just go easy, man! Roy's kickin' up a helluva stink over you killin' Ben Slade. Says you went too far; it could've been settled without guns.'

'Should've told Ben that, he went for his first.'

'Yeah, well you have plenty of witnesses to that.'

'Bardon alone?' When McAdam shook his head slowly, the deputy said, 'Let me guess, Commissioner Lyon's with him — right?'

'And Roy, still fuming. Come on, you'd better not keep 'em waitin'.'

★ ★ ★

McAdam's description of Ashley Lyon — 'Built like a hogshead' — was about as accurate as you could get.

That's what Hunter thought, anyway, when he faced the sweating, red-faced disapproving commissioner, flanked either side by Bardon and Roy Severin.

'No need for you to stay, Mac,' Bardon said tersely. 'Be obliged if you'd finish Hunter's shift for him.'

McAdam frowned, started to speak, but saw Hunter just as the man shook his head slightly. 'Whatever you say, Will.'

No one spoke until after the sheriff had left the room. It was Lyon who spoke first, in a surprisingly rich voice: he had a head round as a ball, a pudding-like face, but mean, mean eyes set deeply. He turned these upon Hunter now.

'So you're the notorious Hunter. You seem to be living up to your name, mister — hunting trouble — *and* blowing it out of all proportion.'

'I don't stand still when a man's pointing a loaded gun at me, Commissioner.'

Lyon's blubbery lips tightened and he frowned at Bardon, who swiftly picked up the hint.

'I'm afraid that's been his attitude all along, Commissioner. Competent, but ruthless.'

'I'm surprised you've retained him as a deputy — the man's a killer! *Likes* to kill, it seems to me. If I may poke my nose into your affairs, briefly, Councillor, I would recommend that he be fired immediately! He's not in the least suitable for a deputy's position in a town we hope to hold up as a fine example to others just starting to flourish.'

Bardon, grim-faced, nodded. (But he was mighty glad to hear Lyon say that about Cimarron — 'to hold it up as an example to others'. Those words held a lot of promise.)

'Consider it done, Commissioner. Your badge, Hunter, and the sooner you leave this town the better.'

'What, no show for the commissioner? Damn! And I spent all that time, practisin'!'

Bardon looked suddenly surprised, flustered, and looked quickly at the big rancher. Roy's face was kind of concerned, too, but suddenly brightened. He shook his head very briefly, and the movement only deepened Bardon's frown.

'Yes,' the rancher said, heavily. 'A pity Commissioner Lyon won't get to see your incredible accuracy with a rifle,

Hunter.' He paused and looked steadily at Bardon. 'But you did impress the whole town, and you'll have to be satisfied with that, you agree, Will?'

Bardon's face had brightened at last as if he had suddenly understood some kind of message the rancher was sending him. *Everyone already knew how good Hunter was with a rifle — and that was the important thing.*

'Yes! Yes, it is a pity, but he's already demonstrated what an incredible marksman he is and, truth known, I was having second thoughts about including Hunter's little act, anyway.' He turned towards the puzzled-looking Lyon, and smiled. 'I heard about your reputation for being a man of peace, Commissioner, and that you had recently introduced a law in Santa Fe that no firearms were to be carried within certain areas of the town. We respect your views, sir.'

'I appreciate that. You see, very recently a young woman was struck by a stray bullet when two cowboys, the worse for drink, of course, decided to settle their differences with guns in a crowded street, no less! No, I am not very impressed with any kind of firearm, used for so-called peaceful purposes or not.'

Bardon looked relieved and Roy said, 'It's an ill wind they say, huh, Will?'

The councillor silently agreed: Lyon was far more righteous than they had allowed and something like Hunter putting on a shooting show at this time would be a mighty big minus when the commissioner came to give his decision about head tax or even ownership of the pass.

They still had that obstacle to conquer.

It was a distinct possibility that Lyon's administration could — would — take over the pass.

And that sure was not in Bardon's plans.

13

Nowhere to Go

'Hear they're kicking you out.'

McAdam was leaning against the door of Hunter's room, watching the man throw his few belongings into his saddle-bags, and buckle the straps on his bedroll.

Hunter told him briefly of what had occurred in Bardon's office.

'Strange that. At the beginning Bardon didn't want to hire you, then suddenly he's all for it, sung your praises after that demo you gave with the dum-dums and the apple coring — then later I got the impression he wanted rid of you again. Figured you must've upset him in some way.'

'It'd be easy enough to do, but I don't recall anything special — except the gunplay, of course.'

McAdam was still frowning. 'How did Lyon react?'

'All for getting rid of me — 'Killer Deputy' — you know. Bardon fawned and agreed, then brought up how good I am with a rifle again. There's somethin' there I'm missin' — all this emphasis of my shootin' ability.'

'Yeah, well he has been hammerin' away at it. Everyone and his brother knows how good a shot you are. Not that you don't deserve the praise, but, seems a mite . . . odd the way he stresses it. I mean, we've other *good* shots in the town, includin' your old *amigo*, Ollie Revell, when he's sober — none as good as you, though.'

Hunter shrugged, straightening, and tossed his bedroll into a corner. He turned to the sheriff, holding out his right hand. 'Been good knowin' you, Mac. And Mrs Mac.'

'You're not going yet! Hell, you've been busted up and look like a hoss stomped you! Wait a spell longer.'

'Always the same with me — I get

fired, I go, no matter when. I'll camp out along the trail. Better air there than in this cramped coffin, anyway.'

Mac threw a glance around the room, looked up at the ceiling, the tower somewhere above there in the darkness. 'Yeah — kinda creepy in a way, too. Stay in touch, *amigo*.'

They shook hands and went downstairs. Hunter paused, wondering whether to look into the kitchen where lights still burned and Tess and her staff were frantically cooking mountains of food for the picnic tables tomorrow.

He decided not to bother. He felt she would be another happy to see him go.

At the livery, Lester, half-empty bottle clutched in one fist, told him he could spend the night in the stall again if he wanted to, offered him a swig. He started to shake his head, but took a slug of the fiery whiskey — Lester's own recipe. 'Kerristopher! That's powerful!'

'Meant to be.' The livery man added,

swigging, 'Looks like rain ... man might's well get wet inside as out, eh?'

Hunter decided to take up the offer of the stall for the night, but refused any more liquor, his head already swimming. 'Thanks, Lester, I will doss here. Stiffer and wearier than I figured.'

'Yeah, I've given myself night shift — no one'll bother you.' His speech was getting very slurred, as he jiggled the gurgling bottle.

A wave of weariness surging through him, Hunter dumped his gear, stifling a yawn and dropping his bedroll which would act as his pillow. He slid his rifle out of the roll straps and lay down with a grunt.

He was asleep in minutes, right arm cradling the weapon loosely down at his side.

Too bad he was so tuckered out — if he'd been just a little more alert it might have saved him when they came for him. He might have heard Lester snoring off his moonshine on a pile of hay, anyway, or the stomp of his disturbed horse.

One of them eased the rifle gently from under his arm and it slid from his weak grip without waking him, except for a muttered sound that might have meant anything.

Then Ollie Revell held the Winchester close to the lantern one of his companions held, turning it this way and that.

'Just look at this mother, will you! I'm a pretty good shot at the best of times but reckon I could hit a groundhog's ass from fifty yards with my eyes shut, usin' this!'

'Come on, Ollie! We gotta get outa here,' a lanky man said anxiously.

'Yeah, OK. Stretch, get his hoss and you get the saddle, Blink, gotta make it look like he left town.'

Then Ollie reversed his hold on the Winchester and casually drove the brass-bound butt against Hunter's head. Blood oozed from his forehead.

'Sleep tight, you son of a bitch!'

For good measure Ollie kicked him

in the ribs, bent and picked him up with a grunt as he draped Hunter over one shoulder. Then walked silently into the night.

★ ★ ★

It was pitch black in the corner where they had dumped him and covered him with an old blanket.

He was bound hand and foot, with a gag tasting like old musty boots in his mouth — not that he had ever willingly had musty old boots in his mouth, some remnant of levity in the back of his aching brain reminded him.

He half-coughed — maybe it was a choked-off laugh — though he sure as hell didn't feel like laughing.

His head was full of an avalanche roaring that didn't diminish and his body felt like he'd fallen off his horse and been dragged for a mile or two. His eyes rolled, filled with tears of pain.

It came back to him slowly how he had been in the livery stall with his horse and — well that was the last he remembered. But he felt a snake of sticky, half-dry blood down one side of his face and neck, coming from over his right eye, and recognized the throbbing of a gun-whipping or simply a vicious slug with a gun butt.

There was no more. He managed to kick the blanket off but he still had no idea where he was or what was happening to him, or what was *going* to happen to him.

There had to be something he was being kept for — otherwise they'd have killed him.

'Halfway feels bad enough,' he mumbled against the stinking gag, trying to ignore his churning belly.

He dozed but fought the urge to drop into a full sleep. *It could be one he'd never wake up from.*

His trying to recall what had been happening did nothing to ease the pain in his head and, finally, he spiralled down into a grey gloom that was neither quite sleep nor quite full consciousness.

For many years he had lived by his instincts and something was telling him now that he was being kept alive for something particular. He had no idea *what* but the knowledge sat solidly and he found he was starting to relax, very slowly, but getting there, until everything was totally black.

★ ★ ★

When he finally opened his eyes and a blade of sunlight seared across them, making him squint, he jerked his head, and managed a grunt of surprise as he saw where he was:

Back in his room on the upper floor of Tess Deacon's rooming-house, sun coming through a gap in the slats above.

What the hell! His mind couldn't cope with the answer mostly because he didn't know it.

But he was lying awkwardly at the foot of the cavity that held the slats that led up to the cramped 'nest' above, one leg bent under him — and not painlessly, either.

Warm blood trickled down his face and dripped from his chin, in a very thin line.

He was still bound and gagged but his body throbbed with new pain as if he had been thrown down the steps and —

Then he heard the voice — somewhere outside, quite strong, quite emphatic in its delivery of words he took a couple of minutes to savvy.

'Cimarron could be an important town to this state, but, ladies and gentlemen, you — the population — have considerable — er — growing up to do!'

The voice was that of Ashley Lyon and it boomed around the buildings in such a fashion that Hunter, through all his aches and pains, realized the man was giving a speech from the platform outside the county offices. This must be the tail end of the *High Noon Howdy*: Lyon's summing-up of his visit here and ready to deliver any decisions he had made.

Then someone — presumably in the gathered crowd, a corner of which he could just see — called out, 'Commissioner, we grew up durin' the war like a lotta other folk in this part of the country! We ain't kids! Say what you wanna say — we'll savvy it — and let you know what we think!'

Other voices concurred, quite loudly, and Lyon let them settle down before saying, almost matter-of-factly, 'I fully understand that and how you people must feel about my coming here from the hallowed halls of Sante Fe . . . ' He paused: perhaps expecting some sign that his feeble attempt at humour was accepted, but, if so, he was disappointed. He went on more sternly, 'I know and understand a lot more about Cimarron, *and* its people, than you may realize. I am pleased that your cattle spreads will now have an easier trail to the meat markets' — a-half-hearted cheer — 'but our problems lie with the pass.'

There were sounds that could have been edgy murmurings, giving the notion that the crowd was far from enamoured with the commissioner and his speech.

Then someone called belligerently, challengingly, 'That's our own doin'! We sweated blood to make that pass and we aim to use it! As our right!'

'Damn right there! Save us hundreds!'

'We'll even pay a light head tax, it's so important to us!'

'Yes, yes, I understand.' Hunter was surprised at the amount of bellowing Lyon could get into his voice. 'It's a very important subject. *But*, it is also *illegal*!'

He allowed the yells and catcalls to die down — and it took some time.

'We have strict ordinances and state laws in Santa Fe — new, I grant you, but copies have been distributed and your town council not having received one yet cannot be accepted as a good or legitimate reason for some of your citizens — well-intentioned as they may be — going ahead and blasting a new road, and, in doing so, without proper engineering supervision, possibly weakening the natural stone walls above the trail. If they were to collapse — '

'The hell! There was no other way.'

'Them walls are harder than a damn politician's heart!' *That one got a good laugh, even a small cheer.*

'And a whole damn more reliable!' another voice added: this time the cheer rang through the square.

There were similar protests before Lyon, sounding a lot more impatient now, bellowed, 'Permission was never even requested from Santa Fe! It was a blatant disregard for the type of law and order we intend — *intend*, I say — to see as the foundation of this developing state!'

A silence as the crowd must have seen where he was going now.

'Give it to us!' a man bawled. 'Forget all the legal hogwash and so on, tell us what's gonna happen!'

'Yeah! Get right to it — we're listenin'!'

There was a ragged backup to this and when it started to dwindle, Lyon said, sounding quite unafraid of any hostile result — and he must have known it *would* be hostile, 'So in my capacity as land administrator I have decided that there *will* be a head tax on all cattle using the pass.' There was silence: obviously the crowd wanted to know how much.

Lyon skimmed around the cost, but dropped a mighty big rotten egg when he said, 'Whatever amount is decided upon, will go straight into Santa Fe coffers for the future development of our state! Oh, yes, it is a penalty for disregarding our laws, but the money will be put to the best possible use. Take a little time and I'm sure you'll agree.'

Hunter had enough sense back now to know that Bardon and Roy Severin would be throwing those 'seven fits to Sunday' that McAdam had mentioned a little while back. They must see their dreams of an easy fortune sliding away faster than a slithering rattler in a forest fire.

Then above the roar and now somewhat frightening mood of the crowd there came another sound, cutting shockingly through the racket: the unmistakable whiplash of a rifle shot.

A sudden silence in the square below. Then screams and men shouting, a few words easily intellegible:

'Goddlemighty! Someone just shot the commissioner!'

Then above Hunter, he saw a pair of legs as a man swiftly descended from the cramped room in the tower. It was Ollie Revell and he held Hunter's rifle, a small curl of smoke still at the muzzle. He grinned at the man at his feet.

'Nice shootin', Hunter! That dumdum near took the sonuver's head off! Too bad you were clumsy tryin' to get away an' fell and hit your head . . . you murderin' bastard!'

As he spoke, Ollie's skinning knife

slashed through the bonds at Hunter's wrists and ankles. Ollie stooped and gathered them up just before the rifle butt cracked against Hunter's mighty sore head again.

Through a long, roaring tunnel he heard Ollie give one final chuckle, then clatter away from this assassination point.

Then, nothing but blackness. Again.

14

Assassin

There was utter chaos in the town square.

People ran in all directions, some wanting to get out of there, find cover in case the sniper started picking random targets. Others were shouting for the sheriff and anyone else in authority. Calmer ones called for a doctor, though it was easy to see by the gore and the absence of most of Commissioner Ashley Lyon's head that a doctor would be of no use.

Some sat or stood wide-eyed, stunned — those down front of the crowd mostly, closest to the platform — looking in horror at the splashes of gore that had reached them and spotted their clothes. One woman had fainted clear away — there was a smear of red down one side of her face — and friends and kin were trying to revive her.

Doctor Earls took one look at the somewhat disgusting heap of flesh that had been the land administrator and began making notes for the coffin maker: it would need to be of special construction to take such bulk.

Sheriff McAdam was there and Ollie Revell came hurrying up, sweating, looking anxious.

'Holy Joe! What happened, Mac?'

McAdam merely gave him a look; it was too obvious a question to bother answering.

'My God! What — what did that to him?' a man in the forefront asked, looking quickly away from the stump of the dead man's head.

'Looks like the work of a dum-dum to me,' Ollie said, leaning forward interestedly. 'Yeah, that's what I'd say. Like Hunter was usin' on them bits of log — Oh-oh!' He turned to McAdam who was watching him closely. 'Hey, Mac, you . . . you don't think — '

'No I don't.'

Ollie spread his hands, but looked dubious. 'Well, it's just that everyone knows he was bein' kicked out of his job an' he *did* have dum-dums and is a top shot with a rifle.'

And suddenly, Sheriff McAdam knew now why Bardon had kept harping on Hunter's accuracy with his Winchester — driving it home so that everyone within earshot knew, and would remember, at a time like this. A fine marksman with a rifle!

Plus, Lyon had made a point of dismissing him from the chief deputy's job. If they had set up Hunter for this — and it was a distinct possibility — especially in the light of Lyon's speech about the pass and the head tax going directly to Santa Fe, *someone had to protest — and loudly!*

He turned to the pressing crowd — those with a strong stomach. 'Did anyone see or hear where the shot came from?'

Several men answered, Ollie Revell's

voice among them. They virtually all said the same thing.

'Up there! Like from Rosa's old tower. That's what it sounded like to me.'

McAdam looked and nodded: a perfect line with the dais.

'Anyone actually see the rifle? Ollie?'

'Don't ask me! Hell, I *heard* the shot and I reckon that's where it came from, but I din' see nothin'.'

Nor did anyone else or, leastways, they weren't admitting it. The assassination of a high government official was something to stay well away from.

'Hey!' Ollie Revell said suddenly. 'Weren't Hunter mixed up in some sort of assassination down in Mexico? Seems I heard that . . . '

Will Bardon had arrived earlier and had stood there listening and now he stepped forward. 'Ollie's right! This Hunter, this *killer* deputy we made the mistake of hiring was involved in some political assassination in Mexico.'

'Hogwash!' snapped Sheriff McAdam.

'It was some wild bunch he was runnin' with after the war and they were cleared. Turned out to be nothin' to do with them at all.'

He didn't know that that was strictly correct, but he was betting Bardon and his friends, like Roy Severin, didn't either.

'Still, that sort of thing sticks to a man,' the big rancher said and Bardon nodded grimly.

'That — and Hunter's killer instinct — plus his markmanship.'

He let it hang and Bardon suddenly asked, looking around, 'Well? Has anyone seen Hunter?'

'I thought he cleared town last night,' spoke up Ollie. 'Leastways, I think Lester or that kid he hires mentioned his hoss and gear had gone.'

'He din' clear town,' spoke up Larry Deveroux, Bardon's head clerk. As all eyes turned towards him, Larry added, 'I seen his horse in that clump of trees by the river bend, not far from my house. Figured he might've camped there for the night.'

'By God! That doesn't sound like the actions of an innocent man!' exclaimed Will Bardon. 'Here, Larry, take some men and check out the town.'

'Try that damn tower of Rosa's,' chimed in Ollie Revell on cue. 'I reckon that's where the shot came from.'

And, of course, they found the near-unconscious Hunter groping at the foot of the slat ladder, holding a bloody head, his eyes glazed and uncomprehending.

By then a white-faced Tess Deacon had joined the small crowd on her second floor and pushed her way on to the balcony. She looked at the groggy Hunter in surprise at first and then in contempt.

'So! You just had to live up to your reputation! And damn you for doing it in my house!'

'Well, here's the rifle,' Roy Severin said, levering. 'And there's still at least one dum-dum in it.'

'He must've fallen in his hurry to get

away,' someone suggested and Revell came in again.

'In a hurry, I guess, or just so damn excited about blowin' Lyon's head off he missed a step and knocked hisself out.'

'Doc! Doc Earls!' Sheriff McAdam called over the rails. 'Come on up here. We got a man hurt and I think he needs to be conscious to defend himself.'

'*Defend* himself?' echoed Revell. 'Judas, where you keep your brains, McAdam? *He's the goddamn killer!* A blind man can see that.'

'Yes, Ollie, it does seem . . . obvious,' Bardon said, trying to sound expansive and fair-minded here. 'It does look bad for our ex-deputy, but — Ah, here comes the doctor now. Take a look at his head, Doc. Could he've got that knock on his skull from a fall?'

Doc Earls knelt and probed, bringing groans from the now semi-conscious Hunter who struggled as the pain knifed through him. 'Yes, of course — But — Yes, I suppose a fall did it.'

'What were you gonna say, Doc?' asked McAdam taking the medic by the upper arm.

'I said it.'

'No, you said somethin', but it wasn't what you started out to say. Come on, Doc. A man's life may depend on your opinion here.'

'You bet it does!' Ollie said and Roy Severin, peered closely, adding, 'It seems pretty clear. He shot Lyon through the slats, turned too fast up there in that cramped spot and stumbled on the slats, banging his head,'

'Doc?' McAdam stared coldly into Earls' flushed face.

'Yes, it could've been that way.'

'But?' asked McAdam, those eyes still boring into the agitated medic.

'Well, there're two wounds here. One older than the other, but apparently made by the same object. Or falling on the same object. See? Here above his eyebrow. A curved cut and the blood flaking — dried — at least for some hours, I'd say, even overnight. This other wound at his hairline is more recent but with the same curved laceration.'

'Like from a rifle butt?' asked McAdam grimly, bringing heads snapping around to glare at him.

'Well, it just could be.'

'What the hell you tryin' to do, Doc?' demanded Ollie Revell. 'Make out Hunter never shot the commissioner?'

'I'm just giving an honest opinion as a practising man of medicine, Revell. I would bet my reputation that those two wounds were made at least hours apart, with the same instrument, or, by a very strange coincidence, falling twice on the same object. And I do not see anything here that could have made such wounds.'

Earls, with Tess who had brought a bowl of warm water, had been cleaning up the wounds while speaking and it was easy for those in the front now to see how similar the cuts were.

'Rifle butt,' McAdam said confidently. 'Hunter's been slugged. Where is that Winchester of his, anyway?'

He took the rifle handed to him by a bystander and turned the butt over. There were pinkish smears on one end of the curved brass butt binding, some congealed blood caught in the slight groove between the brass and the walnut stock.

'My God!' breathed Doc Earls. 'I know blood when I see it! And see this flake? It's skin. Another here with a part of a strand of hair — the colour of Hunter's.'

'The hell're you saying, Doc?' Will Bardon demanded hoarsely, his eyes narrowed.

'I'm not *saying* anything except that this man has wounds made by the same object — at two different times. I think anyone here would have to agree that it would be just too imaginative to say he tripped twice and landed on the same object — '

'Could've happened.'

All gazes turned to big Roy Severin at his words. He spread his hands.

'Couldn't Hunter have come up here, say last night — to check out his shooting angle and so on? Tripped in the dark on the way down and hit whatever it was he hit after trying to get away today?'

Bardon looked as if he wanted to grab the rancher's big hand and shake it. 'Hell, yes! That's a distinct possibility! You have to agree, Doc.'

'It is possible, of course, except I still don't see any object that would've caused wounds of that nature.'

'Only the butt of Hunter's rifle,' said McAdam flatly. 'And *if* Hunter — supposing he's the guilty party — did make a test run last night — surely Tess would have heard him clattering as he fell?'

He looked at the girl quizzically and she frowned, spoke slowly. 'I don't much care for Mr Hunter, but — well, my helpers and I were here baking and cooking until late. I know I didn't hear anything — the other women may have — we can ask, but I have to say we were making considerable noise with pots and pans being used and washed and used again and food scraps taken out to the trash pile. No, I don't think we would've heard if anyone was up here. Hunter had moved out at my request when he was fired from the deputy's job.'

Bardon looked relieved. 'Well, it probably happened that he did have a dry run and tripped.'

'Stretchin' a long bow that he hit his head twice on — well, on what?' demanded McAdam.

'Coulda landed on the rifle butt, couldn't he?' Ollie asked blandly.

'*Twice!* Ollie, you've got some imagination!'

'I din' imagine hearin' that rifle shot above my head earlier!' Revell snapped. 'I know the sound of it from when I shot it myself — '

'And when the hell was that?'

Ollie actually jumped as McAdam virtually roared the question. 'Ollie, Hunter wouldn't even let me handle that gun. I'm damned if he would let you near it, let alone shoot it!'

Bardon and Roy glared coldly at Revell and Ollie licked his lips. 'Aw — all right. I never shot it. I was just sayin' that, but only because I *know* I heard the damn gun shoot and then seen Lyon's head explode like a melon.'

Someone retched in the crowd and there was a scuffle as the man with the weak stomach lurched away.

'Hey! Look, he's comin' round!'

Hunter was moving slowly, blinking, moaning as consciousness returned — no doubt with a thundering headache. He started when he saw the crowd, looked blankly at McAdam.

'What's up, Mac? Ah, Judas, what happened?'

'As if you didn't know, you goddamn killer!' growled Ollie, getting in early.

He drew back a boot and McAdam hit him in the mouth sending him stumbling among the crowd. His hand was almost resting on his gun butt as he said coldly, 'Just get up and stand still,

Ollie! I'll get around to you shortly.'

'Get around to me! Hell, I can't tell you nothin' but that I heard the shot and found this son of a bitch sprawled here with his damn rifle still smokin' beside him.'

Hunter, still gathering his bruised senses, frowned. 'Smoking? I never fired my rifle or any other gun.'

Ollie managed to get most of a kick in this time, but Hunter grabbed the boot and twisted savagely. It wrenched a cry of effort from him but Ollie, caught off balance, spun and crashed against the rail. He started back up, going for his gun and McAdam reached out almost lazily and slammed his Colt across Ollie's head. His hat flew off and he dropped to his knees, clapping both big hands to his head.

'That's enough, Sheriff!' snapped Bardon. 'The hell is the matter with you? Ollie's trying to tell you what he witnessed, and you almost knock him out.'

'Because he's lyin'!' snapped the

207

sheriff. 'Hunter never shot Lyon.'

'What!' Hunter exclaimed. 'Lyon's been shot?'

'Had most of his head removed by one of your dum-dums — ' McAdam told him and Ollie chimed in groggily, holding his head, 'From your rifle.'

That silenced Hunter and he held his own head in both hands, starting a little when he felt Doc Earls' bandages on his head. 'Someone want to tell me what's goin' on?'

'Haw, haw, haw!' snorted Ollie Revell, looking his hatred on McAdam before turning it on Hunter. 'Biggest killer we've ever had in our county and now he's tryin' to say he knows nothin' about shooting Commissioner Lyon! Aw, puleease!'

Hunter's shock turned to alarm as some of what he had seen and heard began to meld — and nudge him with the knowledge that *he* was the murderer in this deal — and it looked like the whole damn town believed it.

Except for McAdam.

And maybe Tess? Well, she was looking kind of uncertain.

But, under her cold stare, as Ollie wouldn't be silenced and kept shouting Hunter's guilt, he saw Tess's face gradually harden.

She believed it too, finally.

15

Dead Man's Gun

The crowd was reluctantly dispersing, almost everyone talking, some folk hesitating as they went off, pausing to give Hunter one last look. The doctor was down on his knees in front of him, holding his eyelids up one at a time, repeatedly, examining them through a magnifying glass.

Doc Earls said, without looking up, 'The eye pupils are slightly different sizes which means he probably has concussion, which may be mild now but worsen later.' He glanced up at Sheriff McAdam who was busy fending questions from some of the crowd while urging them to disperse. 'Sheriff, where are you taking this man?'

'Have to be jail, I guess, Doc.'

'Well, I would be negligent if I

allowed Hunter to be thrown into a cold and dirty jail cell — he would not be under my observation. Concussion is one of those things you can't afford to take chances with. Put him in my infirmary.'

'Infirmary!' a woman echoed, outraged.

Tess, who had just arrived, added, 'Doctor, the man's just killed Commissioner Lyon in a-a horrible manner! He must be kept under lock and key, surely!'

'A court can decide that, Tess, but I will not risk a jail cell this early. Overnight may well be long enough for me to decide about the concussion, so he *will* spend that time in my infirmary — Sheriff?'

'Infirmary's fine with me, Doc. You mind if I kinda camp there, too?'

'I think I would prefer it.'

★ ★ ★

'Who gave Earls permission to put Hunter in the goddamn infirmary!'

211

Will Bardon's voice thundered through the shadowy council chambers where several of the councillors had retreated out of the hot sun. Lyon's ugly corpse had been taken to Doc Earls' Funeral Parlour, a gunny sack covering his shoulders, still dripping blood. Roy Severin looked just as angry as Bardon as he glared at Foster McAdam.

'Not a matter of permission, Will,' the lawman explained evenly. 'It's followin' doctor's orders. Hunter has to have rest and quiet, in case of complications.'

★   ★   ★

'Jesus Christ!' breathed Roy Severin. 'We have a cold-blooded assassin here and we're mollycoddlin' him! We have to show Santa Fe — and mighty quick, too! — that we're movin' on this thing, getting it cleaned up, pronto! Hell, Lyon was a *commissioner*! Not a goddamned janitor!'

Bardon waved a hand almost languidly. 'We're moving, in the right direction, Roy! We haven't put a foot wrong so far and I don't intend that we shall. There'll be a mighty great to-do in Santa Fe and they'll put all the blame they can on us.'

'Don't see how they can do that,' Roy said. 'I mean Hunter was one of our deputies and he turned out to be a callous killer. That's the way we gotta play it.'

'Which we are doing! He killed four men, remember? So we convinced Commissioner Lyon to *fire* Hunter, who, being the grudge-bearing type' — Bardon paused, spreading his hands — 'got square in the only way he knew: with a bullet.'

'Yeah, I reckon Santa Fe will accept that, but we've got to give 'em Hunter — dead, of course. In the jail it would be a simple matter to arrange — '

'If I know Hunter, he won't miss a chance to attempt a breakout.' Bardon kind of sneered, adding, 'But he doesn't have to be successful!' He glanced quickly at the rancher, smiling crookedly.

Severin nodded. 'A known killer, shot while trying to escape. What could be simpler? Happens all the time.'

★ ★ ★

Hunter lay doggo.

It wasn't too hard — his head throbbed and beat like Sioux wardrums gone mad. His face felt sticky with half-dried blood and the remnants of more, only partly washed off; he was mighty uncomfortable.

But at least he wasn't handcuffed or bound, gagged or blindfolded. So all his senses were operating, even if not at full level. He turned his head slowly — and not painlessly! — neck sore and stiff, brain feeling loose in his skull. He could just make out McAdam's bulk sitting in a shadowed corner, smoking silently. *Where the hell was he . . . ?*

'How many ahead of me?' he asked hoarsely, causing the sheriff to jump up and hurriedly come to stand beside the bed.

'What'd you say?'

'How many're ahead of me — for the firin' squad?' His voice was little more than a whisper.

Mac tensed. 'Easy, you're not in that place, feller, that was long ago. This is Doc Earls' infirmary. You know me. Here, look closer.'

Hunter stared, frowning for quite some time and in the end the lawman lit a lamp although it was still only mid-afternoon. He let the warm light wash over his dusty face.

Still Hunter stared, not saying anything, though his breathing had quickened noticeably. His gaze moved jerkily over McAdam and beyond to the infirmary walls.

'Your wife still make great flapjacks?'

McAdam grinned. 'Mebbe she'll do you some for supper! You're startin' to come good.'

'If this is good, glad I don't remember bad.'

Mac chuckled, 'Stay calm. Doc's got somethin' in mind for you.'

Hunter lay there, one hand lightly roving over the bandages and his cut head. 'Hoss throw me?'

Mac shook his head. 'I better remind you — and then start makin' plans to get you outa here.'

* * *

The doctor brought him a vile-tasting glass of cloudy liquid and ordered him to drink it.

Hunter looked suspicious, sniffed and jerked his head back, coughing, a few tears reddening his eyes. 'Judas Priest! What is it? Hoss liniment?'

Earls smiled wearily. 'It has many names — including a lot worse than horse liniment, but its medical name is *sal volatile*. Spelt that way but pronounced *sal vo-lat-lee*. A trusted and very good stimulant for the whole system. Drink it, Hunter, you'll be glad you did, I promise you.'

The raw ammonia content burned his tongue and throat. The alcohol was

216

a pleasant surprise. He made hoarse gasps afterward, blowing out his cheeks, as if he had run uphill a mile.

He found enough breath to cuss the sawbones thoroughly, but broke off as they both stared at him, wearing wide grins. McAdam winked. 'I think it worked, Doc!'

'Seems so,' confirmed the medic. 'It tastes so awful it wakes up anyone but a dead man. Seconds are available, Hunter . . . '

Doc Earls pursed his lips and wriggled his eyebrows as Hunter suggested what he could do with a second dose.

Minutes passed and then he said with some surprise, 'Damn! I-I do feel more chipper compared to a few minutes ago.' He rubbed his chest lightly. 'Think I'll live.'

'You'll be tired again in a minute. Just let it happen and try to relax until tonight, then be ready for — '

'Ready for what, Doc?'

Ollie Revell grinned tightly as he

lounged in the doorway leading back into the main part of Doc Earls' house, thumbs hooked in his gunbelt. 'Maybe he thinks he could get away before he's dragged off for trial?' He paused, pursing. 'Mind, a lotta folk're riled that he brung this down on our town. Did hear a necktie party mentioned in the saloon.' He rubbed his big rough hands together briskly. 'Now that'd be somethin' to look forward to, eh?'

Ollie laughed as he turned and left, closing the door behind him very quietly.

'We've got to get him outa here!' It was an obvious remark and Doc Earls didn't bother to answer. 'Doc? He-he's driftin' off! Thought that stuff you gave him was s'posed to get him up and runnin'?'

The medic lifted a hand slowly. 'I hope everyone thinks the same.'

The sheriff frowned. 'You mean it won't?'

'If it *was* sal volatile alone perhaps it would, but that draught was a special mixture and will not only put him to sleep, he'll lie there as if dead — a condition I will enhance with an injection, plus a few yards of bandage wrapped tightly around his chest.'

And he proceeded, taking a hypodermic needle containing pale-brown liquid and baring Hunter's left arm.

'Well, hell! That's damn convenient! We've got to move him! And he'll be like a damn corpse.'

'Complete with coffin — or rather that box in the corner which is what I use to transport deceased patients to my funeral parlour.'

McAdam stared at the battered grey-wood box, as long as a coffin, but merely an oblong shape. He had seen it being carried into Doc's funeral parlour many a time.

Then he grinned. 'You cunnin' old so-and-so!'

'There'll have to be a few more — er — trimmings, to make it believable, such as skin pallor and restricted head movement. Simple matters, but I'd best get started.'

'Oh-oh! Gonna be awkward, god-dammit!' McAdam growled, as half-a-dozen rough, booze-smelling cowboys came filing in.

'What the hell're you men doin' here?' the sheriff snapped, hand close to gun butt. 'This is an infirmary and — '

'Mr Severin sent us. Let you get some sleep, Sheriff,' spoke up a man Mac knew as Mort Regan: a tough top hand from Lazy S who had been in many a fight and done a short time in jail. 'We'll watch Hunter an' make sure he's tucked away all nice and secure. You fellers can go on back to your old women — er — sorry, men! I mean your *wives*.'

The cowboys laughed and Mac saw how each one kept hands close to their guns and that they weren't as boozed up as they had first seemed.

'Ah, we got us a fine collection here, Doc!' Mac allowed, squaring up to the ranch hands. 'Pick of the bunch!'

'Well, they might as well go away.'

Doc Earls glared sullenly at the staring group.

'The boss told us to stay here, Doc,' Regan said tightly.

'Well, stay if you want, but neither Sheriff McAdam nor myself will be here — ' That brought puzzled looks and a few remarks. 'There's no point — Hunter died about three minutes before you arrived. Oh, look like that if you will, but there he lies, ready for transport to my parlour.'

'How the hell could he just up and suddenly die?' Regan demanded.

'That's the way most folk die. In Hunter's case, I'm sorry to say I missed the fact that he had a fractured skull, not simply concussion. There wouldn't've been much I could do for him, anyway, but no doctor likes to admit to such a thing.'

Mort Regan swaggered forward, frowning, a hand wrapped around his gun butt. He leaned over the coffin-box on its low wooden stand.

'Hell, he looks bad! Grey as this old

wood — Yaahhh! What's that stink, Doc? Phwaaah!'

'The humours of death, Mr Regan — and there is no humour in my saying that. You see, in some people the tissues decay within a very short time and occasionally the bowels — '

Regan had pulled his neckerchief up over his mouth and nose and waved a hand in the medic's face. 'Get him the hell outa here! *No!* We'll get the hell out. Reckon we'll just wait to see him laid away on Boot Hill standin' in the fresh air.'

The cowboys clattered away, coughing, and McAdam held a neckerchief to his own face. 'My God, Doc! Did what you said really happen?'

Earls smiled and reached under the box, bringing out a stone bottle without a stopper. 'We call it *assa-fe-tida* — or sometimes essence of sweaty feet — that's being polite because it — '

'Yeah, yeah, I know what it really smells like!'

Mac scrubbed his face hard as he

moved right away. 'Poor old Hunter! If he wakes up and smells that . . . ' Then alarm. 'He is gonna wake up?'

'Oh, yes, and when he does he will find he's in my funeral parlour. The shock may just bring back full consciousness with a rush — and I rather fancy Mr Hunter will need full consciousness quickly. We'll have to get him moved across as fast as we can now. Can you get some help?'

'Sure, but it won't be dark for another hour.'

'We have to move him where folk can see for themselves that we are tranporting a corpse — or a reasonable facsimile thereof. Please get a move on — I have to give him another injection and it takes a little time to work and bring him out of the induced state I've put him in.'

The door opened and a young man came in who Mac recognized as the clerk from Bardon's store. He looked around wildly, frowned and put a hand across his mouth and nose.

Earls was just sliding the lid on the coffin and the clerk crossed himself, lips moving in a brief prayer.

'Mr Bardon said to tell you gents that he would very much like to see Deputy Hunter laid away before sundown. He has some of Mr Severin's men digging a grave in the cemetery.' The young clerk was already backing out of the infirmary. 'He'll be expecting you, he said.'

'I'll just bet!' McAdam breathed. 'I don't suppose I could find anyone willing to be deputized. Look, we can't take him out there, Doc!'

'That does seem to be out of the question, but what's the alternative?'

'Why don't you ask a dead man?' a voice slurred.

McAdam felt his face drain of blood as Hunter struggled to sit up in his cramped box, hair awry, wild-eyed.

'Goddlemighty! He *does* look dead!'

Earls smiled. 'Think I did a rather good job, don't you?'

* * *

There was a small group of rubber-necking townsfolk already waiting down at Boot Hill behind the town's only church. Another group followed, not getting too close.

Some looked curious, others quite nervous, but all were determined to see the man who had upended their town laid away in this fresh-dug grave under a marker yet to be made. But someone had already chalked words on an old plank stuck in the grave mound: they seemed to echo the mood of the townsfolk of Cimarron:

Here Lies Hunter, a cold-blooded murderer who brought death and terror to our town — no Peace by request!

Then there was a clatter of hoofs and the Lazy S men Severin had sent into town earlier, arrived — including Ollie Revell, eyes glazed with hard drink.

He sat his restless mount, looking arrogant and confident now. 'We want the lid taken off that there box, Doc Earls!' Ollie yelled. His ranch-hand companions roared their agreement and some of the crowd gave half-hearted support.

Ollie and his men had dismounted, except for Piddlin' Pete Cosgrove — the nickname referring more to his manner of betting on cards than how his bodily functions performed. He bit a hunk off his chaw of tobacco, folded his hands on the saddlehorn and set his mount right, slap-bang alongside the coffin-box. He spat some juice as he drew his sixgun, cocked it and aimed it at one of the large thumbscrews holding the lid in place.

'You shoot at that coffin, Pete, and you'll be seein' the inside of my cells for a damn long time!' Mac snapped.

Ollie Revell answered. 'Aw, Mac, you don't seem to realize that you've had the run of this town far too long. Council asked me to tell you you're out of a job which I aim to slip into!' He winked at the staring crowd now.

Someone chuckled — just one person. 'Now, folks, *I* reckon there's a *live* body in there . . . ' He let go with a wild Rebel yell and shot three times through the flimsy lid, splinters flying, Doc throwing up his hands in despair.

Sheriff McAdam lifted his gun at blurring speed even as he said, 'I warned you, Ollie!'

But Piddlin' Pete's gun fired and Mac was slammed forward in his saddle and over the side, almost on his mount's neck. Women and children were screaming now, running away from the graveside — helped willingly enough by their menfolk as the sheriff thudded to the ground.

The doctor, stunned for only moments, knelt swiftly beside McAdam and, even as he lifted his head, he saw four of Roy Severin's men crouching as they fanned their gun hammers. The hail of lead splintered and knocked the coffin box off its stand, the shattered lid falling off — revealing a box packed with old clothes and used-up bedrolls . . .

The shooting stopped and Ollie cursed, started forward, but stopped dead in his tracks as Hunter appeared from behind some bushes, holding his rifle.

Revell dived sideways, shooting desperately as the rifle lifted. In midair his body jerked and spun. He landed on his head, neck snapping, so that it was later debated whether a bullet killed him or the broken neck. Pete Cosgrove disappeared in a hurry, running, yelling.

Hunter turned his smoking gun on to the now scattering Lazy S, jerked his head as a bullet zoomed past his ear. Instinctively he dropped to one knee, cold, calculating eyes streaking around the graveside — and seeing Roy Severin, bringing up his gun for another shot. Hunter worked the rifle's lever in such a blur that afterward folk weren't sure how many times he fired but, later, someone reckoned they dug five slugs out of Big Roy.

Will Bardon, pale as a ghost from one

of the nearby graves, literally threw his sixgun into the air, thrusting his hands as high as he could reach.

'Don't shoot! Don't — shoot — me! *Please!*'

'Wouldn't think of it, Bardon. You're gonna be a valuable man when the enquiry starts into Commissioner Lyon's death — a real valuable man.'

The ruddy sundown gave the whole scene a bloody aspect which seemed appropriate. Long, canted shadows of headboards and gravestones added to the weird scene.

Two men Mac had gathered held Bardon while the others disarmed Roy's hard-cases, taking their guns while Hunter limped hurriedly towards where Doc Earls knelt beside Foster McAdam.

'Doc . . . ?'

Earls glanced over his shoulder, hands bloody where he worked on Mac's wound. 'Body wound. I think he'll recover — in time. Could you stay on a while . . . ?'

Hunter knelt and looked down into

Mac's grey face.

'You're . . . still my . . . deputy — far as I'm concerned,' the sheriff gasped, starting to cough and Earls pushed Hunter unceremoniously aside.

Hunter grinned. 'For you I'll do it, but don't get any ideas it's gonna be permanent — I'm still a long-ridin' man.'

* * *

Ten days later, his gunhand still tingling from the strength of Mac's farewell grip, Hunter turned up Cedar Street and slowed his mount as he came to Tess's rooming-house. She was hanging out some washing and he rode up slowly.

He knew she had heard him, if not seen him, but she didn't turn. 'On my way now.'

No reply, nor did she turn her head.

'Thought you might like to give a farewell cheer or somethin'.'

'Goodbye is all I'll say.' An indifferent tone as she sought some pegs to pin up a dripping blanket.

'I like the wide open spaces, long miles to ride. I might be back this way some time.'

She glanced coolly at him and, as he shrugged and began to wheel his horse, she said, 'There's nothing for you here, Hunter, there never will be!'

The words hurt but he covered it well, touched his hat brim in a two-fingered salute. 'Then I guess it's *adios* and good luck!'

He nudged the claybank and set off at a canter.

When he was just out of earshot, she whirled, sucked down a deep breath, but the words came as little more than a whisper. 'And to you, Hunter. To you too!'

The last was barely audible and she rubbed irritably at the touch of sudden moisture on her cheek.

There was a wind getting up so probably it was just a little water blown off the wet blanket.

Probably.

We do hope that you have enjoyed reading this large print book.

Did you know that all of our titles are available for purchase?

We publish a wide range of high quality large print books including:
Romances, Mysteries, Classics
General Fiction
Non Fiction and Westerns

Special interest titles available in large print are:
The Little Oxford Dictionary
Music Book, Song Book
Hymn Book, Service Book

Also available from us courtesy of Oxford University Press:
Young Readers' Dictionary
(large print edition)
Young Readers' Thesaurus
(large print edition)

For further information or a free brochure, please contact us at:
Ulverscroft Large Print Books Ltd.,
The Green, Bradgate Road, Anstey,
Leicester, LE7 7FU, England.
Tel: (00 44) **0116 236 4325**
Fax: (00 44) **0116 234 0205**

GUN STORM

Corba Sunman

Death comes calling on the small mining town of Lodestone when the storekeeper's wife Martha is murdered by a thief. Deputy Jim Donovan pursues and guns down a man witnessed fleeing the scene, but testimony from his brother Joey indicates that the killer is still at large. Elroy Johnson, the stagecoach robber Donovan arrested three years ago, is back in town — could he be involved? Meanwhile, the outlaw Stomp Cullen and his gang have been spotted lurking around Lodestone. All signs point to an upcoming gun storm . . .

SKYHORSE

John Ladd

Judge Nathan Berkley requests a seemingly simple task of his adopted son, Appaloosa King: ride to the remote town of Deadlock to pick up Catherine, the judge's newly-discovered daughter. Trouble starts when, on the way, King leads his two cowboys off on a diversion, aiming to meet up with a mysterious messenger — who, unbeknownst to the trio, has a deadly reason for the rendezvous. All looks lost until a stranger arrives on the scene — the man known as Sky-horse . . .